Haunted Schools
True Ghost Stories

ALLAN ZULLO

Rainbow Bridge®
Troll

To Anna Wartowski, who is such a remarkable teacher,
it's downright scary.

Copyright © 1996 by The Wordsellers, Inc.

Published by Rainbow Bridge, an imprint and trademark of Troll Communications L.L.C.

Cover design by Tony Greco & Associates.
Cover illustration by Kersti Frigell.

Printed in the United States of America.

10   9   8   7   6   5   4   3   2   1

Library of Congress Cataloging-in-Publication Data

Zullo, Allan.
Haunted schools: true ghost stories / Allan Zullo.
p.   cm.
"Rainbow Bridge."
Summary: Nine stories about ghosts and phantoms found haunting schools.
ISBN 0-8167-3837-8 (pbk.)
1. Ghost stories, American.   2. Children's stories, American.
[1. Ghosts—Fiction.   2. Schools—Fiction.   3. Short stories.]
I. Title.
PZ7.Z82Hau   1996   [Fic]—dc20   95-30296

CONTENTS

The Stay-Behind 7

The Ghost from Never-Never Land 19

The Twelfth Man 33

The Kissing Ghost of Rosemont Academy.....47

Screams of Horror, Cries of Terror 63

The Phantom Graduate 76

The Curse on Missy Green 89

The Scene-Stealer...103

The Red-Rock Spirits....................................114

DOES A GHOST ROAM IN YOUR SCHOOL?

Ghosts have appeared in all sorts of places, such as graveyards, caves, haunted houses—even schools! Kids have reported seeing phantoms in big new schools, old one-room buildings, and fancy academies.

In many cases experts were called in to investigate these so-called hauntings. Usually the experts walked away baffled. All they knew for sure was that something weird had happened that could not fully be explained.

This book is a creepy collection of stories about spirits haunting everything from classrooms to a playground to a school library. You will read nine eerie tales inspired, in part, by real-life cases taken from the files of noted ghost hunters. The names and places in the stories have been changed to protect everyone's privacy.

Does a ghost roam in your school? You might think so after reading the spooky stories in this book!

THE STAY-BEHIND

In a clearing atop a wooded hill the old one-room schoolhouse didn't so much stand as it did lean. The peeling wood siding had last been painted much too long ago for anyone to remember. Many slats of the black shutters that covered six big windows had fallen off from rot. On the peak of the rust-stained tin roof a weather-beaten bell tower was on the brink of collapse. Yet it still housed a cast-iron bell whose ring faithfully had announced the beginning of the school day for generations of kids who grew up in nearby Chandler's Hollow.

In 1953—after serving the community for more than 60 years—the school was closed. Although people in the area didn't have the money to preserve the building, they refused to tear it down. They left the school as it was, with desks, bookcases, and a slate blackboard still in their places, although just about everything else was cleaned out. The community wanted to keep the schoolhouse as a reminder of the days when kids of all ages were taught at one time, under one roof, by one teacher.

It was in this aging, abandoned structure where Troy

Anders and Cody Kincaid received a school lesson they will never forget.

Troy, 12, a big-city boy, was spending much of the summer with Cody, his 13-year-old country cousin. One day the two rode bikes on a remote gravel road to a spring-fed pond. On the way they passed the old schoolhouse.

"It's been empty for years and years," explained Cody.

"Can we go inside?" asked Troy.

"It's locked. There's nothing much to see. Just an old big dusty room. People say it's haunted."

"It is?" Troy asked excitedly.

"Yeah, I guess so. Mary Alms, who lives on the farm up the road, says she's heard voices—kids laughing and stuff—when she's come by here. Melvin McCarr was out with his hounds one night, and they pitched a howling fit when they came near it. Melvin says he walked up to the schoolhouse and saw lights flickering through the shutters. He checked the door, and it was locked. So then he peeked through one of the shutters and saw an older woman inside.

"She wore clothes from 50 years ago and was sitting at her desk reading to a couple of barefoot kids in their seats. The dogs were making a ruckus, so Melvin turned around to hush them up. He noticed the dogs' hair was standing on end. Melvin got them quieted down, but when he looked back in the schoolhouse, it was all dark inside. Lots of people have seen or heard spooky things inside."

"Wow!" said Troy. "Have *you* seen any ghosts?"

"Nah, I don't believe in them," said Cody. "Come on, let's head over to the springs and cool off. It's hotter out here than the inside of a chicken coop at high noon."

Within minutes Cody and Troy were splashing in the crystal-clear water. After an hour of fun they toweled off when a loud clanging sound echoed off the surrounding hills.

"What's that?" asked Troy.

"Sounds like a school bell. But there isn't any school for miles around, except for the old empty one. Let's go check it out."

They hopped on their bikes and followed the ringing, which led them directly to the schoolhouse. When they reached the school yard, Cody looked up at the bell tower and said, "That bell is ringing its darn fool head off. Someone must have broken in." They walked up to the door, but the padlock was still clasped to the latch. After circling the building and finding that all the shutters were closed, the boys wondered how anyone got inside.

Cody stepped back from the school to get a better view of the bell tower. "I don't know what to make of that," said Cody, pointing to the bell. "There's no rope, nothing to make it move. But it's ringing on its own!"

"You did say it was haunted."

"Some people *claim* it is. Let's go inside."

"But it's locked."

"No problem." Cody pulled out a pocket knife, and in minutes the lock snapped free. At that exact moment the bell stopped ringing. A twinge of nervousness spread through Troy's stomach. For Cody, the bigger and tougher of the two boys, curiosity was building with each passing second.

"Let's see if we can solve the mystery of the bell." He pushed open the squeaky weathered door, and they stepped into a large room where the stale, musty air caused the boys to sneeze. Thin beams of light from the afternoon sun squeezed through the shutters' broken slats, casting an eerie glow on the room's contents, which were covered in dust and laced with spiderwebs. Facing a teacher's simple oak desk were four rows, each with six wooden straight-back chairs. Each chair had an arm on the right side only that flared out into a foot-square pad upon which the students would write.

Troy sat in one of the chairs. "Man, are these uncomfortable. Can you imagine sitting in one all day? Ouch, my back would stay sore for nine months a year."

"Yeah, and with the arms on the right side, I feel sorry for all the students who were lefties."

They began looking at all the small letters, names, and dates that had been carved in the chairs over the years: K.L. + A.A . . . 8/24/32 . . . Kilroy was here . . . BOO.

"What about the bell?" Troy asked.

Cody looked up through the opening of the ceiling to the bell tower. "I don't get it. Without a rope there's no earthly reason for the bell to be ringing."

"Well, I guess we should go," said Troy, feeling a bit jittery about the bell.

With every step they took, the wood flood creaked and groaned. About 30 feet (9 m) from the door, a wood plank snapped under Troy's weight, and his left foot plunged through a hole in the floor. "Ow! Hey, Cody, my foot is stuck. Help me out."

Cody chuckled as he kneeled down and pushed the broken plank out of the way, freeing Troy. Before he stood up, Cody spotted an object inside the hole. He reached down and pulled out a thin book small enough to fit into a pocket.

"Troy, look at this!" The worn book was so old that the lettering on the cardboardlike cover had nearly faded away.

They could barely make out the title: *Cobb's Juvenile Reader.* About 100 delicate pages, yellowed from age, were bound to the spine by string and still readable.

"Be careful with this book," cautioned Troy. "It could be valuable."

The boys were so intent on examining their find that they failed to heed a new sound coming from the front of the room. TAP, TAP, TAP.

They looked up in surprise. Standing by the teacher's desk was a husky woman in her early sixties, hitting the top of her desk with a wooden pointer. Her brown hair was rolled up in a bun, and a pair of rimless eyeglasses, attached to a chain around her neck, were perched on the end of her nose. She wore a long, flowered dress and a pair of plain brown shoes.

"You boys are tardy," she gently scolded them. "You know what they say: 'Lost time is never found again.'"

Troy and Cody stared at her in openmouthed amazement, not moving a muscle. The book slipped out of Cody's hand and fell to the floor.

"Find your seats now so we can get started," she said.

"Pardon me, ma'am, but just who are you?" asked Cody.

Flashing a patient smile, the woman replied, "Why, I'm Miss Sissy Simmons, of course." The way her tongue drew out the *s*'s of her name reminded the boys of the hissing sound a snake makes.

"How did you get in here without us seeing you?" asked Troy.

"I've been here the whole time," she answered. "You probably weren't paying attention, that's all."

"But when we came in," countered Cody, "the room was empty."

"Oh, but you're wrong. I'm here. I've always been here."

11

She flicked her wrist. "Now enough of this dillydallying. We have much to cover today."

Cody cocked his head. "Pardon?"

Miss Simmons put her hands on her hips and huffed, "'Dost thou love life? Then do not squander time, for that is the stuff life is made of.' Words to heed from *Poor Richard's Almanac*. Find your seats now, please. We have lessons to do."

"Cody," Troy whispered out of the side of his mouth. "Is she insane or what? Maybe we ought to split right now."

"She's a little touched in the head," Cody agreed. "But let's play along and see what happens."

The boys dutifully sat in chairs across from each other in the middle of their rows. "Good," said Miss Simmons. "Today we're going to talk about states and their capitals, work on our division, practice penmanship, and read." Pointing to Troy, she added, "But first, why don't you lead us in the Pledge of Allegiance."

This is stupid, thought Troy. *I can't believe I'm here, pretending to be a student for this crazy lady.* He glanced at Cody, who gave him a wink. Slowly he and Cody stood up, and Troy started, "I pledge allegiance to the flag of the United States . . ."

When they finished and sat down, Miss Simmons said, "Doesn't it seem awfully dark in here? I think the shutters should be opened." The boys heard creaking noises, and saw the room brighten from streams of sunlight.

"The shutters!" yelled Troy. "They're opening by themselves!"

"How did you do that?" Cody asked the woman.

Miss Simmons dismissed the question with another flick of her wrist and said, "Now let's get out *Cobb's Juvenile Reader.*"

The boys were so spooked by the unexplained way the shutters opened that they gazed blankly toward the front of the room. Finally Troy warily raised his hand. "Uh, ma'am, Miss Simmons, we don't have our books."

She shook her head. "You're new here, aren't you? Look on the floor behind you. You'll find a *Cobb's Reader* that you two can share. Now turn to page 45 and begin reading out loud."

Cody picked up the book he had dropped, returned to his chair, and opened the reader. After scooting his chair over toward Cody, Troy turned to the page, cleared his throat, and began reading from a page titled "What Is Pleasant":

"'It is very pleasant to walk in the fields and to have the sun shining wherever we go. There are some people who would like to have nothing but summer, and who wish that the days were always long and bright, and that there were no cold wind, or snow, or winter nights.

"'Without snow or rain, the seeds from which the flowers and the fruits of the summer spring up, would perish and never do any good.'"

"You were superb," praised Miss Simmons. Pointing to Cody, she said, "Now you read to the class."

Trying to mask the growing uneasiness in his voice, Cody mumbled and read as fast as he could: "'It is a sad thing to have learned to read, and not to know that a pretty book is better than a ball or a kite or any toy in the world. For a toy, you know, is soon spoiled or we grow tired of it, and then we forget it, and it's no use. But a book can tell us many kinds of things, and contains sometimes pretty stories.

"'So when the winter comes again, do not be sorry, but ask your papa or mama to find some pretty book, in which you will read of things of which you will be pleased to know.'"

When the boys looked up from the book, Miss Simmons was gone.

"Where did she go?" asked Troy.

"She must have sneaked out while we were reading this book. Man, that is one weird lady."

"Let's go before she comes back and tries to give us another lesson." Troy shoved the book in his back pocket, and they started for the door.

"Just where do you think you are going?" It was Miss Simmons, her arms folded, standing in front of the door. "Get back to your seats, please."

Suddenly the room filled with children's laughter—the kind directed at a classmate in trouble.

"Where's the laughter coming from?" asked Troy, his eyes growing wider by the second.

"From inside this room," Cody replied, his head turning in search of the source. "But there's no one else except you, me, and the crazy lady."

"Boys, sit down!" Miss Simmons ordered. "Don't let me have to use the switch on you."

Totally bewildered by the laughter, the boys meekly returned to their seats.

"Now then, who can name me the states that begin with A?" she asked.

When the boys remained silent, Miss Simmons marched over to Troy and whacked her pointer on his desk. He winced and rattled off, "Alabama, Arizona, Arkansas, and Alaska."

"The first three are correct," said Miss Simmons. "But Alaska is not a state. It's a territory."

"Ma'am," said Troy. "Alaska is our 49th state."

"Land sakes," she said with a chuckle. "How many states do you think we have?"

"Fifty."

"And the other is?"

"Hawaii."

"No, Hawaii is a territory too," she stated.

"That's it!" snapped Cody, rising out of his chair. "The fun is over, ma'am. This has gone on long enough. I don't know how you pulled off that trick with the shutters, and I don't know where you came from. But we're not reading from any more little books, and we're not playing your pretend games. We're leaving. And, by the way, there really are 50 states. Look it up yourself."

"What?" she said, her eyes glaring. "Do you think you can simply walk out of school whenever you want?" She gazed over their heads and then addressed the empty chairs, "Well, children, can we just leave whenever we want?"

Out of nowhere came a chorus of *no*'s and *uh-uhs*.

"Where's that *coming* from?" said Troy, his throat tightening. "I don't see any kids, do you, Cody?"

"Time to get out of here!" Cody shouted.

BANG, BANG, BANG, BANG, BANG, BANG.

The boys froze and watched in shock as the shutters slammed shut—by themselves—one after the other. By the time the boys recovered, the door had closed too.

"Now see what you have done," hissed Miss Simmons, her eyes flashing angrily. "The whole class must be punished for your behavior."

A collective groan filled the room, and a chorus of boos and nasty remarks rained on the befuddled boys. Nothing made sense to Troy and Cody—the strange woman or the voices of invisible children laughing at them.

Miss Simmons strode down the middle row of desks and announced, "We will sit in darkened silence and pray that the evil thoughts and deeds you have brought forth will be cleansed from your minds and mouths."

With his teeth clenched, Cody whispered to his cousin, "I don't know about you, but I'm busting out of here." Troy nodded. "On the count of three. One, two, three—go!"

The boys shoved a few of the chairs aside as they scrambled for the door Miss Simmons was guarding. "Just shove her out of the way, Cody!"

With their heads down, the boys charged the woman—and then barreled right through her! They whipped open the door and sprinted outside into the sunshine.

"What just happened?" asked Cody.

"I know it's impossible, but we ran straight through her! I mean, it was like she wasn't even there, but she was there. We saw her."

"I don't get it either. Let's go!" They hopped on their bicycles and sped off toward home, pumping furiously until they were a mile away. They finally took a break near a weed-infested cemetery.

"Who was that woman, Cody?" asked Troy.

"I don't know, but I think we were in the presence of a certified nut case. How she pulled off those stunts with the shutters and the disappearing act is beyond me."

"Can you imagine having a teacher like Miss Sissy Simmons?" asked Troy, mocking her by exaggerating the s's of her name. They both laughed. But then Troy dropped his bike on the side of the road and stared past Cody. "Oh, man, this is too creepy."

"What is?"

As if in a daze, Troy walked past Cody toward one of the gravestones. "Cody, look at this!" he said, his voice rising with excitement. With a shaking hand he pointed to the words etched in a gray granite tombstone:

Sissy Anne Simmons
Beloved Teacher
1888-1949

Suddenly the afternoon quiet was shattered again by the pealing of the school bell. The freaked-out boys jumped onto their bikes and pedaled straight home. Within 24 hours everyone around Chandler's Hollow had heard about the boys' encounter with the ghostly teacher.

Curious adults and children held vigils at the old schoolhouse day and night, waiting for Miss Simmons to show up again or for something spooky to happen. But nothing did.

About a month later Karl Heller, a noted ghost hunter, heard about the case and arrived in Chandler's Hollow to investigate. He interviewed the boys and talked to other people in the area who previously claimed to have seen or heard strange things at the schoolhouse. Heller also spent several days inside the building.

When he finished his investigation he told Cody, Troy, and the townspeople his startling conclusion: "I believe you boys encountered what I call a 'stay-behind.'

"Most ghosts are people who died tragically and are unable to recognize what happened to them," Mr. Heller explained. "They move about in the physical world, but usually not outside the immediate area of where they died.

"However, many ghost sightings involve people who had peaceful deaths. Upon further investigation, I found these cases all had two things in common—the people were strong-willed and greatly attached to their surroundings before their deaths. They are the stay-behinds. They are spirits aware of their own death who won't let go of their former surroundings. They're simply unwilling to leave their earthly surroundings even though they no longer possess a physical body. Stay-behinds are still capable of causing bizarre phenomena, especially if they can draw on the energy of other people.

"In the case of Sissy Anne Simmons, she was a teacher in Chandler's Hollow for nearly 40 years, according to what I could find in the archives of the school board. Apparently she never married and gave all of herself to that one-room school. She died in that building at the age of 61. I believe she loved that school so much that her spirit wanted to stay. She became a stay-behind."

"Why did we see her, and others haven't?" asked Troy.

"Like a typical stay-behind, Sissy Simmons is quite satisfied to continue living her former life, staying out of the way of real people. She remains undiscovered until someone with special ability notices her by accident, or unless a real person comes in contact with something that was dear to her when she was alive. In this case she appeared after Cody found the book. In other cases, for unknown reasons, the stay-behind wants people to know he or she is still around. Obviously Sissy Simmons wanted to teach, and you two happened to be her students for the day."

"I've had some unusual teachers," said Troy, "but no one like Sissy Simmons!"

THE GHOST FROM NEVER-NEVER LAND

Matty Rankin didn't know why, but she had a sneaking suspicion that the new girl who showed up at the school playground was not who she claimed to be.

She definitely was different from the other kids. Maybe it was the girl's clothes: the sleeveless yellow blouse with the rounded Peter Pan collar, the short green plaid skirt, the puffy white socks, and the laced-up Buster Brown shoes. The clothes reminded Matty of those her mother wore as a child. Maybe it was the girl's hairstyle: pulled back in a ponytail with bangs in the front, and bright yellow plastic barrettes on each side of her head, holding her brown hair in place. Or maybe it was her eyes: big, dark ones that never looked at you, but rather through you.

Matty had met the new girl the day before during recess after lunch at Pineview Middle School. Kids were playing freeze tag and kickball and seeing how long they could bounce a soccer ball on their head.

Matty and her good friend Lacy Sundberg were jumping rope when the new girl suddenly appeared at the playground.

"Hi," she said. "Can I jump rope with you?"

Matty nodded at Lacy and said, "Okay."

"Hi, my name is Wendy."

"I'm Matty Rankin and this is Lacy Sundberg. You're new here, aren't you?"

"Yes," Wendy replied. "My family moved here from Los Angeles."

"Welcome to Pineview," said Lacy. "We're in the fourth grade. What grade are you in?"

"I'm in fourth too. I haven't been enrolled yet. My mom is going to take care of that soon."

"Where do you live?" Matty asked.

"In the Northwood area."

"Northwood?" said Lacy. "That's where all the fancy mansions are."

"Uh-huh. We have a big house. It's got four bedrooms, each with a bathroom, and all of us kids have our own room. And we have a playroom with all kinds of games. It's neat."

"That sounds cool," Lacy said.

"Is Carrie McIntyre in your class?" asked Wendy.

The girls shook their head. "We've never heard of her," said Matty. "Oh, the school bell is ringing. We've got to go now. Bye."

As Matty and Lacy strolled into the school, their teacher, Mrs. Jordan, stopped them and asked, "Who was that girl you were jumping rope with?"

"She's new, Mrs. Jordan," Lacy replied. "Her name is Wendy, and she moved here from Los Angeles."

"Really? Hmmm." Mrs. Jordan glanced out at the playground but no longer saw Wendy.

"How are you feeling today, Mrs. Jordan?" Matty asked.

"I didn't have a headache all morning, but I feel a bad one coming on," replied the teacher.

From the time she was a girl, Mrs. Jordan had suffered from terrible headaches called migraines. Although she learned to control them with medication, the headaches grew worse after she transferred to Pineview at the beginning of the school year.

"Girls, if my headache gets any worse, I'll probably get cranky and send all of you down to the office," she said with a grin and a wink.

The next day at recess Matty and Lacy were jumping rope at the playground when Wendy showed up again.

"Hi, Wendy," Lacy said. "Are you enrolled yet?"

"I'm in Miss Bassetti's class," replied Wendy.

"I don't know her," said Matty. "There are only three fourth-grade classes—Mrs. Jordan's, Miss Watson's, and Mr. Suarez's."

"My teacher is Miss Bassetti," Wendy insisted. "Can I jump rope now?"

Matty and Lacy each took an end of the rope and began swinging it as Wendy hopped into the middle. Matty and Lacy then began a chant, linking the names of Wendy and the cutest boy in their class:

"Down by the river, where the green grass grows
There sat Wendy, sweet as a rose.
Along came Jason and kissed her on the cheek.
How many kisses did Wendy get that week?"

Then they started counting the number of times Wendy jumped rope.

Wendy was nearing 50 jumps when Mrs. Jordan, who was roaming through the playground, spotted her. *I have a bad feeling about that girl,* thought Mrs. Jordan. Suddenly the teacher was staggered by a rush of intense emotions. Inexplicably, she felt a jumble of guilt and sadness. And then another migraine struck her. *What is it about Wendy?* The teacher began walking toward the girl when the principal, Mrs. Foster, called out, "Mrs. Jordan, make sure to pick up the parents' notes in your box. They're supposed to go home with the students today."

Mrs. Jordan turned and said, "I will, Mrs. Foster. Thanks for reminding me." When the teacher looked back, she saw Matty and Lacy, but without Wendy. "Where's Wendy?" she asked them.

"I don't know," replied Lacy, looking around. "She was here just a second ago."

"Did she say what class she was in, Lacy?"

"Yes, in Miss Bassetti's. Is she a new teacher?"

"Bassetti? That name sounds vaguely familiar. But, no, we don't have such a teacher, unless she's a substitute."

Later that day, during reading period, Mrs. Jordan kept rubbing her temples, hoping to ease a throbbing headache. She couldn't get Wendy out of her mind. *I wonder if she's really telling the truth. I think I'll investigate after class.*

After she dismissed her students, Mrs. Jordan went to the office and asked the secretary, Diane Lincoln, "Has a new student been enrolled during the last few days? A girl named Wendy?"

Diane checked her files on the computer. "No. Adam Bird was the last new student, and that was three weeks ago."

Mrs. Jordan then approached Mrs. Foster and warned, "I

think we may have a little problem. The last few days a girl who isn't enrolled in the school has been showing up at the playground and playing with two of my students. She told them she attends school here, but I just learned that she hasn't registered."

"Really? What's her name?"

"Wendy. I don't know her last name. She's about nine or ten."

"Do you think she comes from a home where the parents are keeping her out of school?" asked the principal.

"Maybe. I'll try to get some answers tomorrow if she shows up." Mrs. Jordan started to leave and then said, "Oh, I almost forgot. She told the kids that her teacher was a Miss Bassetti. There's no one here by that name, is there?"

The principal shook her head.

"I didn't think so," said Mrs. Jordan. "But that name rings a bell with me. I just can't seem to place it."

"How are your migraines?" asked Mrs. Foster.

"They've been pretty bad the last few days."

The next afternoon Mrs. Jordan stood outside during recess and waited for Wendy to appear. A few minutes later she spotted the little girl in the same yellow blouse and plaid skirt that she had worn on previous days. Wendy was sitting high on the monkey bars while Lacy and Matty were talking to her from below. The teacher walked briskly toward them. She was only ten yards (9 m) away when Wendy dropped to the ground behind the two girls, who were standing between her and Mrs. Jordan.

"Excuse me, girls, I want to talk to Wendy," said Mrs. Jordan. Matty and Lacy moved aside as the teacher ducked under the monkey bars, her eyes fixed on the back of a brown-haired, ponytailed girl in a yellow blouse. Mrs. Jordan tapped her on the shoulder. "Wendy, I want to talk to you."

When the girl turned around, Mrs. Jordan declared, "You're not Wendy."

"Of course, not, Mrs. Jordan. I'm Hillary. You know that."

Seeing the girl from behind, Mrs. Jordan had mistaken her for Wendy.

"Where's the girl who was on the monkey bars?" asked the teacher.

"I don't know," said Hillary with a shrug.

Turning to Lacy and Matty, the bewildered teacher asked, "Girls? Did you see where she went?"

They shook their heads. "No, she just shows up and then she leaves," said Matty.

"Did she say anything to you?"

"Yes, she said, 'Here comes Carrie.'"

Mrs. Jordan's stomach squeezed into a knot. "'*Carrie*?' Are you positive, Matty?"

"Yes. In fact, she asked about Carrie the other day. Mrs. Jordan, who's Carrie?"

"I can't believe this," muttered the teacher. "How would Wendy know?"

Mrs. Jordan waited in the playground for Wendy the next day, but the girl failed to appear. *I bet Wendy knows I'm looking for her and is afraid to talk to me because I have some tough questions for her*, thought Mrs. Jordan. *She might be staying away from the playground because I'm around.*

The following day in class the teacher called Lacy and Matty up to her desk. "I need your help, girls. At recess, if

24

Wendy shows up, would one of you please come and get me? But don't let her know."

"Is she in trouble?" asked Matty.

"No, nothing like that. But I have some questions for her, and I think she's avoiding me because she's afraid."

"Afraid of what?" asked Lacy.

"I'm not sure. Please come and get me the next time you see her, okay?"

Two days later the girls were playing on the monkey bars when Wendy suddenly appeared. "Hi, Lacy. Hi, Matty."

"Wendy, where have you been?" asked Lacy. "We haven't seen you in a few days."

"I stayed home. My dad was going on a long trip, so he wanted to spend time with me. We played games and hula hoops and watched TV. And we ate ice-cream sundaes and popcorn and soda. We laughed and played bingo and everything. It was so much fun."

Lacy began slowly walking backward. Just as Lacy was about to turn and run toward the school to get Mrs. Jordan, Wendy asked suspiciously, "Where are you going?"

"Me? Um, I have to go to the bathroom. I'll be right back."

"You must really like that outfit," said Matty, drawing Wendy's attention away from Lacy.

"I do. Why?"

"Oh, nothing, just that it's the only thing I've ever seen you wear."

"That's because all our clothes got lost in the move, and we're wearing things we brought in our suitcase. I didn't want my parents buying us all new things, so our clothes get washed every day."

"Are you in school yet?"

25

"Yes, of course. Miss Bassetti's class."

"What room is that?"

"234."

"234? It can't be. That's Miss Watson's class."

"No, it's Miss Bassetti's. I ought to know."

Meanwhile Lacy went searching for Mrs. Jordan. She found her teacher in the nurse's office, lying down with a cold washcloth over her forehead. "She's here!" Lacy announced. "Wendy is at the playground."

"Thank you, Lacy." Mrs. Jordan dashed out of the office and hurried toward the playground. She scanned the area, but failed to see Wendy. She went up to Matty and asked, "Where's Wendy?"

"I tried to keep her here, Mrs. Jordan. I turned away for just a second and then she disappeared."

"Did she say anything to you?"

"She said her teacher is Miss Bassetti in Room 234."

"But 234 is Miss Watson's class." Mrs. Jordan wrinkled her eyebrows. "Hmmm. My class was Room 234 when I was in the fourth grade here years ago."

"Oh, that's right," said Matty. "You once told us you used to be a student here at Pineview."

"What was your name back then?" Lacy asked.

"Carrie. Carrie McIntyre."

"Carrie?" said Matty. "Wendy once asked me if I knew a Carrie McIntyre. The other day when she saw you, she said, 'Here comes Carrie.' How would Wendy know your name?"

Lacy piped up, "Isn't it weird that she'd say she's in Room 234, and it was your room when you were a kid?"

The teacher suffered another flood of guilt and sadness that left her reeling. Her body began to shake. She grabbed the metal tubing on the monkey bars to steady herself.

"Mrs. Jordan, are you all right?" asked Lacy. "You look like you just saw a ghost."

What's happening to me? fretted Mrs. Jordan as she splashed water on her face in the bathroom of the teacher's lounge. *Why do I get such bad feelings of guilt whenever I see Wendy? Where did she come from? Why is she avoiding me? How would she know my maiden name and that I went to this school? I feel like I should know her. But how? And why does the name Bassetti sound familiar?*

Mrs. Jordan had never felt like this before—so tense, anxious, and afraid. She was scared because she knew that hidden in the deepest, darkest corner of her mind, blocked by the tormenting headaches, lurked a terrible memory. Something she did not want to remember.

At the end of the day she walked into the office and said to the school secretary, "Diane, you've worked here longer than anyone. Do you recall a teacher named Bassetti? I was wondering if she taught here when I went to Pineview."

Diane went to an old file cabinet. "Let me look at the old teacher rosters. When were you a student here?"

"Fourth through sixth grade, from 1960 to 1963."

"Bassetti. Ah, here it is! She was a fourth-grade teacher in Room 234."

"That was my classroom. But my teacher was Mrs. Leander."

"Don't you remember? She was Miss Bassetti for the first part of the school year. And then she married and became Mrs. Leander."

"I forgot all about that." Mrs. Jordan's stomach tightened,

and her hands began to sweat. "Diane, do you keep student records that far back?"

"Yes."

"Can you check to see if there was a girl named Wendy in school during any of those years?"

Diane spent a long time checking the class rosters. She came up with nothing. "Not a single Wendy during those years in any of the grades," Diane reported. She looked up at the teacher and asked, "Are you feeling all right, Carrie?"

"No, Diane, I'm not."

"Another migraine?"

"That and much, much more."

Lacy had stayed late after school that afternoon to help decorate the gym for an upcoming awards ceremony. While waiting for a ride from her mother, she went out to the playground, sat on a swing, and began to read a book.

"Hi, Lacy."

"Wendy, hi. Where did you go this afternoon? We were looking . . . I mean, I wanted to play with you. When I came out, Matty said you had disappeared."

"Yes, I know. I didn't want Carrie to see me."

"Carrie? You mean Mrs. Carrie Jordan?"

"Carrie McIntyre."

"How do you know her?"

"We went to school together."

"Very funny, Wendy. How about telling me the truth."

"I am."

"Wendy, I know you don't go to school here. And I bet you didn't come from Los Angeles, and that you don't live in a big house in Northwood. I wish you'd be honest with me."

28

Wendy shuffled her feet and bowed her head. "You're right, Lacy." Wendy sat on the ground in front of Lacy and confessed, "I don't have a fancy house or a big family. In fact, I don't have a family at all. I never knew my dad, and my mom was too sick and poor to take care of me. So I was sent to an orphanage—the Butler Home for Children. You know, the brick building on Buckingham and Third Street a few blocks from here."

"Wendy, you're telling a fib again. That's not an orphanage. It's an office building."

"It's an orphanage," Wendy snapped. "I ought to know. I live there. I made up the story about having a nice family because, well, I wanted one real bad and because all the kids in school talked about their families."

"You don't have to feel ashamed about being in an orphanage."

"That's what Carrie used to say. She was always nice to me, not like some of the kids who made fun of me. They called me Little Orphan Annie."

"Wendy, why would they make fun of you?"

"Because I didn't have nice clothes or a family, and I was poor. Carrie was different from the others. She was my friend. And now she's hurting real bad. I feel her pain."

"She suffers from awful headaches."

"You know why she gets them, Lacy? Because of me."

"I don't understand."

"I've come back to tell her it wasn't her fault. She had nothing to do with it. Everything that happened was entirely my fault. She isn't to blame. Will you make sure to tell her that?"

"Why don't you tell her yourself, Wendy?"

"No, it would be too much of a shock for her. Promise me you'll tell her she's not to blame. If she believes me, then she'll finally be at peace. And so will I."

"Okay, I promise," Lacy pledged, still not understanding what Wendy was talking about.

"Thanks, Lacy," said Wendy, flashing a bright smile. She leaped to her feet and scampered over to the monkey bars. "Do you like *Peter Pan*?"

"It's one of my favorite stories."

Wendy climbed the monkey bars. When she reached the top bar, she stood up as if she were a gymnast on the balance beam and spread out her arms. "I'm Wendy, and I can fly!"

"Wendy, you're scaring me. Be careful. You could fall and hurt yourself."

"With a little magic dust from Tinker Bell, I can fly to Never-Never Land."

"Wendy, get down!"

"Okay," said Wendy. But then an unexpected gust of wind threw her off balance, and the girl fell off the top of the monkey bars. She plunged to the ground with a sickening thud.

"Wendy!" shrieked Lacy. She raced over to the girl, who lay in the dirt, unconscious. Lacy frantically looked around for help, but didn't see anyone. She then dashed into the school and plowed into her teacher in the hallway.

"Mrs. Jordan!" Lacy shouted breathlessly. "It's Wendy! She fell off the monkey bars! I think she's dead!"

"What?" cried Mrs. Jordan. She sprinted to the playground, fearing the worst. But when they reached the monkey bars, Wendy's body wasn't there.

"Where is she?" asked the teacher.

"I don't know. I saw her fall off the monkey bars. She was

pretending to be Wendy in *Peter Pan*. She said she could fly, but then she smashed into the ground. I thought for sure she was dead."

Suddenly the terrible memory that Carrie Jordan had so desperately tried to keep buried all these years burst forth in a torrent of flashbacks: Pineview School. Wendy. The monkey bars. The fatal accident.

Mrs. Jordan fell weakly to her knees and burst into tears. "No! No! This can't be happening again!"

Totally mystified by her teacher's reaction, a frightened Lacy asked, "Mrs. Jordan, what is it?"

When she finally regained her composure, the teacher wiped her tears with the back of her hand and said, "When I was in fourth grade, I had a friend named Annie Merrick, but the kids called her Little Orphan Annie. She lived in an orphanage, the Butler Home for Children, that used to be on the corner of Buckingham and Third Street. It was torn down about ten years ago.

"She made up stories about having a family. When the kids found out she was lying and living in an orphanage, they picked on her. She was so unhappy that she dreamed of being Wendy in *Peter Pan* and flying off to Never-Never Land where she could live a happy life.

"One day I was with her when she climbed the monkey bars at this very same playground. She stood up on the top bar. I warned her to be careful. Annie announced that her name was Wendy, that she had been sprinkled with magic dust, and could fly to Never-Never Land. I begged her to be careful. She was about to come down from the top bar when she fell, broke her neck, and died."

Lacy grabbed her teacher's hand and squeezed tightly.

"Mrs. Jordan! What you described is exactly what I saw happen just a few minutes ago. But before she fell, she told me that you were her friend and stuck up for her and treated her nice. She made me promise to give you a message: She said she felt your pain, and that you aren't to blame. It wasn't your fault. If you believe what she says, you'll both be at peace."

The teacher bit her lip as new tears trickled down her face. "Ever since Annie died, I've felt guilty that I didn't prevent her from falling," Mrs. Jordan explained. "I began suffering from headaches because I tried to put that horrible moment out of my mind. When I grew up and became a teacher, I still had migraines. They got worse when I transferred to Pineview this year. Annie's spirit must have sensed my pain, and she tried to reach out to me through you. You were a big help, Lacy."

"You're saying Annie was a ghost?" Lacy asked, her jaw dropping from astonishment.

Mrs. Jordan nodded, adding, "But she won't be coming back. She did her job. I no longer feel the pain—except in my heart."

The teacher threw an arm around Lacy and walked her slowly back into the school. Later that night Mrs. Jordan returned to the playground alone. She climbed on the monkey bars and whispered, "Thank you for caring about me, Annie— or Wendy, if that's what you want to be called. You always did have the flair for the dramatic. Thanks to you I've finally come to terms with your death. I hope so very much that you're now at peace and have found your own Never-Never Land."

From that moment on Carrie McIntyre Jordan never suffered another headache—except for the minor ones that her rowdy class sometimes gave her.

THE TWELFTH MAN

Johnny "Blue" Edwards yearned to be an athlete. He lived and breathed sports. Unfortunately he was a little too short and a little too chubby. And he lacked one other trait—skill. But what he lacked in talent, he made up in heart and guts.

Every year in junior high and his first two years at Hamilton High School, Blue would try out for football. And every year he would be among the last ones cut. He would have been cut much earlier during tryouts if it hadn't been for his effort and enthusiasm. "You know, Blue," said one coach, "you make yourself so difficult to cut. You have the desire and the attitude. If only you had the skills we need."

"I'll try harder next year, Coach," said the disappointed but determined Blue. "You're not going to get rid of me that easily."

The coaches always found a way to make Blue a part of the team. They named him the team trainer so they could take advantage of his positive outlook on life and his tremendous school spirit.

By the time he got to high school Blue kept working out, hoping to get in better shape. But he was simply too awkward and clumsy. And his body didn't respond well to training. He tired easily and sometimes got dizzy even though he passed his physicals.

During football tryouts of his senior year at Hamilton, Blue knew this would be his last chance to make the football team. So every day he would be among the first out onto the practice field and the last one to leave.

"Blue, why do you work so hard?" asked a friend.

"Because I don't want to be the team trainer anymore," Blue replied. "I want to be a player."

Like so many other times, Blue survived the first two cuts. Two weeks before the first game Coach Phillips picked the team's final roster. The players crowded around the list of names posted on the door outside the coach's office. Blue was all too familiar with the ritual. Most of the boys who saw their names gave a shout of glee and thrust their fists in the air. In the past Blue would work his way through the crowd and then search for his name, hoping against hope that it would be there. But it never was.

This day was different. His eyes scanned down the alphabetical list, five names, ten names, and then he blinked twice. To be absolutely, positively sure, his index finger stabbed directly under each letter of the name on the computer printout: EDWARDS, BLUE.

"Yes! Yes! Yes!" he shouted joyfully as tears of pent-up relief and happiness poured out of his brown eyes.

His best buddy, Jed Leary, the starting linebacker and co-captain, reached through the mob and gave Blue a big bear hug and rubbed his crewcut head. "You did it, man! You finally made the team!"

Other players came up to Blue and slapped him on the back. "Congratulations, Blue!" "Way to go!" "You're a player now."

Coach Phillips singled out Blue and said loud enough for all to hear, "I'm proud of you, Blue. You worked harder than anyone, and you deserve a spot on the roster. Unfortunately we're going to lose the best trainer this school's ever had!"

"But, Coach, you're gaining a linebacker," replied Blue. "And I promise you I'll find a way to help this team win every game," adding with a laugh, "dead or alive."

No one knew then just how true his words would be.

That day Blue practiced with an awesome spirit and energy that surprised even Jed. Blue pounded the tackling dummies over and over and performed drills like a Most Valuable Player. His uniform soaked with sweat, Blue soon became dizzy.

"Hey, Blue, are you all right?" asked Jed.

"Yeah, I'm fine. I'm so pumped because I made the team. We're going to play Twin Lakes High, and I want to beat them so bad I can taste it. They always seem to whip us at the last minute. But this year it's going to be different."

As they headed toward the locker room, Blue put an arm on Jed's shoulder and said, "I know I can make a difference. All I want is a chance to play."

"You will, Blue." Jed stopped when he saw Blue groan and stagger. "Blue, what's wrong?"

"I don't feel so well." And then Blue lost consciousness and collapsed.

Paramedics arrived within minutes to find Coach Phillips

and Jed performing CPR on the stricken player. Blue was rushed to the hospital, but despite the best efforts of surgeons he died an hour later on the operating table. An autopsy revealed he suffered from a serious heart defect that had gone undetected by doctors.

The team was devastated. In fact the entire student body of Hamilton High mourned, because everyone knew and liked Blue. In his honor they wore blue ribbons the day after his death.

Johnny Edwards got his nickname Blue because he loved the color. Ever since he was in grade school, he always wore at least one blue thing—socks, shirt, pants, cap, underwear. It didn't matter. He had to wear blue.

He once kidded Jed, "I'm thinking about transferring to Twin Lakes."

"Why would you want to go to our arch rival?"

"Because they're the only school in the conference that wears blue uniforms!"

Knowing how much Blue loved the color, his parents decided to bury him in his blue suit. At the wake attended by grief-stricken players and classmates, Jed walked up to the open casket and said good-bye. In Jed's hand was the jersey that Blue would have worn.

"Hey, good buddy, I have your uniform—the one you worked so hard to get," Jed whispered while fighting back the tears. "I want it to stay with you." Jed unrolled the jersey and placed it across Blue's chest.

After the funeral the players held a meeting and agreed to dedicate the season to Blue. To show their feelings for him, they decided to wear a blue number 55 on the back of their helmets, which represented Blue's jersey number.

No one took Blue's death harder than Jed. For days he moped around in a daze, unable to accept the fact that his best friend had died so young, so unexpectedly.

"Jed, I need you to get your head back into practice," said Coach Phillips. "I know how difficult it must be for you. But think of what Blue would want from you. He'd be kicking your butt right now and telling you to work harder in practice. And he'd be telling you to beat Twin Lakes."

Jed cracked a smile, the first one since Blue died. "You're right, Coach. I'll be ready for the game. No way is Twin Lakes going to beat us this time."

The night before the game Jed tossed and turned in bed. Thoughts of the upcoming contest set the butterflies in his stomach aflutter. Suddenly he had a weird sensation that he was not alone. Jed rolled over and gasped.

In the corner of the room, bathed in the streetlight that filtered through the window, stood Blue decked out in jersey number 55.

Jed sat up and stammered from shock, "B-B-Blue? Is that really you?"

"It's me."

"I must be dreaming," Jed murmured, still stunned.

"Maybe. But you always did have a problem getting to sleep before a game. Jed, I came to tell you something important: I'll be with you and the team this whole season. Don't ever forget that."

Blue faded away. Jed rubbed his eyes, then flung the sheets off and darted over to the corner of the room where he last saw Blue. *Was Blue's ghost real?* he wondered. *Was it a dream? Do I miss Blue so much that I imagined he was actually here? It had to be my imagination. There are no such things as ghosts.*

The Twin Lakes Rams were a thorn in the sides of the Hamilton Warriors. In the last three games between the schools, Twin Lakes had managed to squeak past Hamilton by scoring the winning points in the final minutes.

The Warriors were determined not to let that happen again. Reminding his teammates that Blue would be with them in spirit, Jed led the players' charge out onto the field for the first game of the season. Playing inspired football, Hamilton's defense stalled the high-octane Rams' passing offense. Jed was playing the best game of his career, making ten tackles, knocking down three passes, recovering a fumble, and twice sacking the quarterback.

The Warriors held a slim 12–10 lead with only two minutes left when they punted to the Rams. It was do-or-die time for Twin Lakes. As the Rams marched down the field with a crisp passing attack against the wilting Warriors' defense, everyone in the stands wondered if Hamilton would lose another heartbreaker.

With only four seconds left, Twin Lakes lined up for a relatively easy 25-yard (23-m) field goal that could win the game for the fourth straight year. Jed waved his arms and jumped up and down, trying to distract the kicker. The snap was perfect and so was the hold. The kicker hit the ball solidly, and it flew over the outstretched fingers of the Warriors.

Jed turned to watch the flight of the ball. His heart sank when he saw it was on target. But amazingly the ball veered off to the left at the last possible moment and fell harmlessly to the ground. The referee signaled no good!

The Warriors had survived a tough, nail-biting 12–10 victory over their rivals. Jed happily ran around the field, hugging his teammates and yelling, "We won! We won!" In celebration the winners jumped on one another in a big pile in the end zone. When they finally untangled themselves, Jed, who was near the bottom, grasped the goalpost to lift himself up.

And that's when he noticed it. Carved in the paint on the goalpost were the letters *JBE* over a vertical mark. *JBE?* Jed wondered. *Johnny Blue Edwards? Maybe he carved this on the day he found out he made the team.*

Jed looked skyward and bellowed, "Hey, good buddy, we won! This one's for you!"

After accepting praise and congratulations from fans who had poured onto the field, Jed hustled into the locker room where Coach Phillips was talking to reporters. "We played a hard-fought game tonight, and our players deserved to win," the coach said. "For once we got a break. That kick looked like it was going to be perfect. Then the ball just lost it. Does anyone know what happened? Did it hit a bird? Did the wind shove it?"

Inspired by the victory, the Warriors clobbered their next two opponents on the road by scores of 31–6 and 23–14.

Looking for its fourth straight win of the season, Hamilton played host to the always tough Woodstock Rockets. Jed struggled during the game, making only five tackles as the Rockets built up a 20–7 fourth-quarter lead.

But Hamilton battled back and scored a late touchdown and the extra point, slicing the margin to 20–14. When the Warriors got the ball back on their own 45-yard (41-m) line, they had used up all their timeouts and had less than three minutes left in the game. Still, they engineered a desperate drive and rambled down to the 12-yard (11-m) line with only 20 seconds left.

Quarterback Lee Lancaster then faded back to pass and looked for a receiver, but he couldn't find anyone open. The clock kept ticking. Fifteen . . . fourteen . . . thirteen. . . He scrambled to his left and dodged the onrushing linemen. He needed to get out of bounds to stop the clock. Twelve . . . eleven . . . ten. . .

He didn't make it. A Woodstock defender leaped on Lee's back and dragged him down. After the tackle Lee sprang to his feet, hoping to get off one more play. But it looked as if time would run out before the Warriors could line up again.

Suddenly the field was cloaked in darkness. The stadium lights and the scoreboard clock mysteriously had gone out! The players stood still, and the refs blew their whistles. Moments later the stadium lights and scoreboard lit up again and the clock began running. The coaches and refs huddled at midfield, where the officials ruled that Hamilton would have time for one more play.

With the crowd on its feet screaming, Lee took the snap for the final play. He sidestepped a would-be tackler and rifled a throw to Donnie Clayton in the end zone for a game-tying touchdown on the final tick of the clock. The crowd went wild. According to the rules, the Warriors were allowed a try for the extra point. Despite the crushing pressure on the kicker, he booted the ball straight through the uprights. Hamilton had won 21–20!

Once again Jed and his teammates piled on one another in celebration of another heart-pounding victory—one that relied on a lucky break for the second time. When the rejoicing died down, Jed ran back to the bench to retrieve his helmet. As he reached down to pick it up, he spotted a blue chin strap on the bench.

He picked it up and examined it closely. *This looks exactly like the one Blue used to wear,* Jed told himself. No one else on the team wore a blue strap because Hamilton's school colors were green and gold. And the Woodstock Rockets wore red and black. *This couldn't be his, could it?* Jed wondered. *But who else would have one? And how would it have gotten here?*

He tossed the chin strap in his helmet and jogged toward the locker room. As he passed the goalpost, he stopped at the base and noticed that four vertical marks had been carved below the initials JBE. Jed figured that someone must have gouged a mark on the goalpost for each win.

Back in the locker room a relieved Coach Phillips told the press, "I talked to our athletic director, and no one knows why the power went out in the stadium. It was another lucky break. I don't think we would have had time to get off another play without the interruption. Someone must be looking out for us."

Jed gazed at the blue chin strap that he had found. *I wonder if Blue isn't that "someone."*

Convinced that they were destined to go undefeated, the Warriors confidently breezed through their next game, winning on the road 28–3. Before a home game the following week, Jed walked over to the goalpost and saw that next to the carved JBE was a slash across the four vertical marks, signifying Hamilton's five wins.

As soon as the next game is over, I'm going to see who's carving the post. That's assuming we'll win. Which we will.

Jed was right. The Warriors won handily, 17–0.

After the final gun sounded, Jed kept his eyes glued to the goalpost as he hustled toward it. But he was distracted for a few seconds when the opposing quarterback shook his hand and congratulated him on a good game. Jed thanked him and then hurried over to the goalpost.

Under JBE a sixth mark had been carved into the paint. Jed looked around to see if he could tell who might have done it. But there were too many students and adults milling around. Then he got an idea.

On Monday morning Jed walked into the administration office and asked to see a list of all the students at Hamilton High. He examined it to see if any student had the initials JBE. Jed found only one—Johnny Blue Edwards.

Over the next two weeks the Warriors won road games by scores of 28–14 and 17–6 to run their unbeaten streak to eight straight. If they could win their final two games, both at home, they would finish with a perfect record and capture the conference championship for the first time in the school's history.

Their next opponents, the Jackson Jaguars, who sported a 6–2 record, proved to be a tough team. Both squads marched up and down the field, battering each other's defense. Midway in the fourth quarter Hamilton held a 35–31 lead. Jed, playing with a painful bruise in his thigh, was not performing at his best. But he refused to come out of the game. It was too important.

On third down and four yards to go from their own 42-yard (38-m) line, the Jaguars ran a draw play that fooled the Warriors. The rusher burst through the line, dodged two Hamilton defenders, and slipped through Jed's grasp. The runner then broke into the clear with no one between him and the goal line. It looked like a sure touchdown. Jed gave chase even though he knew it was hopeless. The runner reached Hamilton's 45-yard line . . . then the 40 . . . the 35 . . . the 30 . . . when, incredibly, he began to stumble. He tried desperately to regain his balance, but he couldn't and hit the ground. He then scrambled to his feet but got smashed to the turf by a flying tackle from Jed.

"Who tripped me?" asked the runner in disbelief.

"No one," Jed replied. "You fell on your own."

"No way. Someone got me from behind."

Jed chuckled. "It was your own clumsy feet." But Jed turned silent when he spotted a blue mouthguard lying in the grass. The only player he knew who wore a mouthguard that color was Blue. Since league rules stated that all players must wear mouthguards, Jed called the ref over and pointed it out. However, the official checked and found that all the players were wearing their mouthguards.

Is it possible Blue did this? wondered Jed. He turned skyward and said half-jokingly and half-earnestly, "Hey, Blue, did you tackle that guy?"

Jed quickly turned his attention back to the game. The Hamilton defense held tight and stopped the Jaguars cold to preserve a thrilling 35–31 triumph. Jed was so excited about the victory that he forgot to check the goalpost until after a midfield celebration. When he walked to the end zone, he found the ninth notch carved in the post.

"I don't know what happened," Coach Phillips told reporters after the game, "but if that player hadn't tripped at our 30-yard (27-m) line, he would have scored the go-ahead touchdown. We probably would have lost 38–35. Boy, we've certainly had the breaks this year."

Yeah, thought Jed, *and I'm beginning to believe that Blue is responsible for all of them.*

It was the night of the biggest game in Hamilton High's history—a conference championship and an undefeated season were on the line. The Warriors needed to whip the powerful 8–1 West High Wildcats.

The Hamilton locker room was unusually quiet before kickoff. Finally Jed broke the silence. "Tonight we have the chance to become champions. We've worked hard and had some breaks go our way. We also had an advantage that no other team has had." Jed held up his helmet and pointed to number 55 on the back. "At every game we've had a twelfth man out there with us. Number 55."

Jed took a deep breath and coughed. He needed to buy a few seconds to keep his voice from cracking because he was filled with emotion. "One of the last things Blue said before he died was that he'd find a way to help this team. He's been with us through this whole season. And I believe he's responsible for all the lucky breaks we've had. I know he's here with us tonight, and somehow, some way, he's going to help us win. So let's go out there and make history!"

The game turned into a defensive struggle from start to finish. Jed was so fired up he made 12 tackles and had two sacks. For the entire second half the Warriors held on to a 10–6 lead. But in the final minute of the game the Wildcats drove all the way down to Hamilton's 5-yard (4.5-m) line. It was fourth and goal with 20 seconds left to play.

The Warriors called their last time out. After getting instructions from Coach Phillips, Jed told his teammates in the defensive huddle, "Our whole season—everything we've ever worked for—comes down to this one play. Who wants it more, them or us? Whatever it takes, don't let them score. Blue, if you're with us, now is the time to help out."

The fans in the stands stomped their feet, the cheerleaders screamed, and the players on both benches shouted encouragement. Here was the play of the season. The fullback took the handoff and, with two blockers in front of him, ran a sweep to the right. One of the blockers knocked Jed out of the way, clearing a path to the end zone when cries of "Fumble!" filled the air. The ball bounced crazily on the turf. Jed, scrambling on his knees, lunged for the ball and grabbed it with his fingertips. Then he brought it into his chest and curled up like a baby while 21 other players jumped on him.

The whistle blew, and the Warriors leaped to their feet, flush with joy. But their happiness was short-lived. The referee had thrown a penalty flag! "Too many men on the field," he declared.

"*What?*" screamed Jed. "Who's the twelfth man?"

"Number 55, the one who caused the fumble."

"Fifty-five? But that's Blue's number."

The other refs pushed the players out of the way while they consulted with the official. They told him they hadn't seen an extra player, so the official admitted he must have made a mistake. He then picked up his yellow flag, waved it over his head, and announced, "There is no penalty. The play stands!"

The elated Warriors then ran out the clock, and bedlam erupted in the stadium. The victors threw their helmets in the air and danced and hugged one another as fans and parents shared in the wild celebration.

An hour later the stadium had all but emptied. Jed, his uniform drenched with sweat and covered with grass stains, dirt, and blood, strolled over to the spot where he had recovered the fumble. He closed his eyes and relived that proud moment. When he opened his eyes, he found a blue wristband in the grass. He picked it up and gingerly held it in his hands.

Tears began flowing as he murmured, "This definitely is a sign, isn't it, Blue? Thanks, good buddy. All year, whenever we were in trouble, you were there to bail us out. You stuck by your promise. We couldn't have won it all without your help."

Jed then walked over to the goal post. Ten notches had been carved under the letters JBE—and the word CHAMPS.

THE KISSING GHOST OF ROSEMONT ACADEMY

Marlee Thompson was sitting cross-legged on her bed, studying a chapter in her chemistry book, when she felt a tickle in the back of her neck. The 14-year-old boarding school student scratched the itch and kept on reading.

She again felt the tickle—like a feather lightly brushing across her skin. This time she scratched a little harder and rubbed her neck. *It can't be a mosquito, because it's the dead of winter,* she thought. *Maybe it's my new haircut. The back of my neck is so bare, I'm not used to it. I knew I shouldn't have cut off that much.*

Marlee was about to return to her textbook when she noticed that the mattress on her bed moved as if somebody had sat on it. And then she experienced the strangest sensation—something cold, wet, and soft pressed on the back of her neck, giving her the chills. She slapped her neck and rubbed it.

Marlee turned around and, in a fraction of a second, caught a glimpse of a young man sitting on her bed. Or so she thought.

Marlee leaped off her bed with a scream and backed away.

Hearing the shrieks, her roommate, Trish Bellamy, who was in the hall, charged into the room, "What's wrong?"

"I—I d-don't know," Marlee stammered. "I was reading in bed and felt someone sit down behind me and . . . this is really going to sound silly . . . give me a kiss on the neck!"

"You've got to be kidding!"

"It gets even sillier. When I turned around I saw a young man for a split second, like someone flashing a picture in front of your eyes. You know you saw something, but you don't know what it was. It happened so fast I couldn't begin to describe him."

"I know what it was," said Trish in mock seriousness. "You have an intense crush on Robby Cooper, and it's affecting your brain cells! You thought so hard about him kissing you on the neck that you actually felt it."

"That's not it at all," scoffed Marlee. "What makes you think I have a crush on Robby?"

"Oh, come on," Trish chided her. "You talk about him all the time. When you see him, you laugh at everything he says, and you're always batting your baby blues at him."

"That's not true! He's a nice guy. Just because he's kind of cute—"

"Kind of? He's *very* cute. It's obvious why you're daydreaming about him."

"Honest, Trish, I wasn't thinking about Robby. I was reading my chemistry book when it happened. I felt spooked. What do you suppose it was?"

"It's just like my biology class," Trish said with a shrug. "I don't have a clue."

Marlee and Trish attended Rosemont Academy, a private

boarding school for girls in grades 7 through 12. The main building was once a sprawling 30-room stone mansion set atop a wooded hill and built at the turn of the century. The family that owned the place, the Endicotts, lost their enormous wealth in the stock market crash of 1929. The mansion remained vacant for several years before it was converted into an exclusive girls' school. Over the years new buildings were added to house classrooms, chemistry labs, a gymnasium, and a music center.

By the 1970s it had earned a reputation as one of the most respected—but strictest—boarding schools in Canada. Enrollment was limited to only 100 girls who had the brains, personality, and talent to pass the difficult entrance exams.

Rosemont girls wore uniforms—navy blue blazer, Oxford button-down blouse, gray wool skirt, navy blue knee socks, and penny loafers. The school had many strict rules, even a policy against too much makeup: only lipstick, a little blush, and mascara; no eye shadow, nail polish, or dangling earrings.

Marlee, born and raised in Vancouver, and Trish, from Montreal, were paired up as roommates when they entered Rosemont in seventh grade. The two were soon dubbed by fellow classmates as the Pixie Dust Twins because they looked so much alike. Both were small for their age and could pass for younger kids. Each had big blue eyes that dominated their sweet faces. And both had curly blond hair so shiny it glistened in the sun.

Marlee and Trish hit it off great and stayed roommates through the ninth grade. That was the year they encountered the shock of their lives—the Kissing Ghost of Rosemont Academy.

✳   ✳   ✳

One night Marlee whisked into their room, closed the door, and braced a chair under the knob.

"Why the secrecy?" asked Trish.

"Look what I've got," whispered Marlee, opening up a large canvas bag. She pulled out a teardrop-shaped piece of plastic. "Do you know what this is?"

"I'm not sure," replied Trish.

"It's a message indicator . . . for this!" announced Marlee, whipping out a thin plastic board with letters and numbers on it.

"A Ouija board!" Trish exclaimed.

"Shhhh! Be quiet. You know we aren't supposed to have one. They're totally banned at Rosemont."

"I know. But we're big girls. If we can use it to communicate with a spirit, what's the harm? Where did you get it?"

"Robby's friend, Kevin Porter, gave it to me. I've got to return it next week when we go to the Brooks School dance."

"Oh, this will be fun! Let's ask it questions."

The girls sat on the floor across from each other and set the board between them. They placed their fingers lightly on the message indicator. At first the girls didn't believe the Ouija board could answer any of their questions. But for the next 15 minutes, as the girls concentrated, the indicator moved across the board seemingly by itself. It answered questions by pointing to the YES and NO marked on the board and to letters on the board, which spelled out words.

The Ouija board told the girls that Marlee would not fall in love with Robby but with K.P. Could that be his friend, Kevin Porter? Trish would eventually marry and have three kids.

Marlee asked the Ouija board if there was a spirit in the room. The girls squealed when it answered YES.

"What's your name?" asked Marlee.

The indicator moved to NO.

"It doesn't want to tell us its name," Trish said.

"Ouija," asked Marlee, "why won't you tell us who you are?"

It spelled out S-H-Y.

The girls giggled. "Oh, it's okay," Trish said. "You can tell us. What's your name?"

NO.

"Are you a male?"

YES.

"When did you die?"

1-9-2-8.

"How old were you?"

1-5.

"How did you die?"

S-T-E-A-M.

"Steam? That doesn't make sense," said Marlee. "Where did you die?"

H-E-R-E.

"Here, in this school?"

B-Y-E.

"Wait, don't go," Trish pleaded. "Will you come back tomorrow night?"

The indicator didn't move. "It looks like the Ouija is done answering questions," said Marlee.

"Wow, that was cool. Do you think any of it was real?"

"Could be. If the Ouija can be believed, a 15-year-old boy died here in 1928. Let's check it out tomorrow at the school library. We should be able to find a history of this place. Maybe that will give us some answers."

"Marlee, what if it's true?"

"Then we're the first Rosemont students to communicate with a spirit from the beyond!"

The next day the girls found only a brief history of the Endicott mansion before it was turned into a school. But it provided information that shot a torpedo through their hopes that the Ouija was correct. Cecil Endicott, who made his fortune as an investor, had a wife, Kate, and two daughters, Nancy and Linda. The girls were in their teens when the family was forced to move out of their mansion in 1930. The history made no mention of any son.

"Well, I guess that proves the Ouija is just a dumb game," Trish said with a sigh. "It doesn't look like anyone died here in 1928."

"I guess you're right. But let's try to contact the spirit tonight and see what he says."

"That's assuming a spirit really exists."

That night the girls brought out the Ouija board again and summoned the spirit. The message indicator was quite lively and moving quickly to answer their questions. Other than refusing to tell his name, the spirit gave the same replies to the questions they had asked the previous night.

"Will you please tell us your name?" Trish begged.

NO.

"Your initials?"

After a long pause the Ouija spelled, H-I-J.

"So tell me, HIJ, are you cute?"

NO.

"Do you think we're cute?"

YES.

"Do you like us?"

52

YES.

"Will we ever get to see you?"

The indicator moved back and forth from YES to NO twice.

"We'll take that to mean maybe," said Trish. "Where can we find proof that you died here?"

N-E-C-E-L-L-A-R.

"*Necellar*—what's that?" asked Trish.

"It's not *necellar,* Trish. I bet it's short for northeast corner of the cellar."

Trish clutched Marlee's arm and pretended to be scared. "Maybe we'll find a body!"

"Or a skeleton!" Marlee giggled. "Ouija, what will we find in the cellar?"

H-I-J.

"We're going to find *you* there?"

B-Y-E.

As they put the Ouija board away, Trish asked her roomie, "So, do you think our spirited friend is actually in the cellar?"

"If so, he probably won't look very cute," said Marlee. "After all, he's been dead for about 70 years."

"When do you want to explore the cellar?"

"Let's try this weekend. Meanwhile, I've got a chemistry test to study for."

"Fine with me, roomie," said Trish. "I'm going to take a shower."

It was a half hour later, while reading her chemistry book, that Marlee experienced her first ghostly kiss. She didn't know what it was at the time. But the girls became more suspicious the next night when Trish received a spooky kiss. It happened after the roomies complained to each other about looking younger than their age.

"How are we ever going to get boys to pay attention to us if they think we're in grade school?" moaned Trish.

"Let's stop pouting and do something about it," declared Marlee, flashing a devilish grin. "Come over here by the mirror. Let's see how old we can make ourselves."

Twenty minutes later they had remade themselves by adding lip liner, eye shadow, and dangling earrings, and by putting up their hair.

"You definitely look older, Marlee—at least, oh, I don't know, maybe 14 ½."

"Well," Marlee retorted, "you look a little older too—like an 80-year-old painted hag!"

Trish snickered, picked up a pillow, and clobbered her roomie over the head. Marlee grabbed the pillow, slammed her back, and then zoomed out the door. As Trish bent down to pick up the pillow, she felt a cold wet kiss on the side of her neck. For a fleeting moment she saw a young man standing between her and the door.

Just then Marlee returned, pointing a squirt gun that she borrowed from across the hall. She was about to pull the trigger when she saw the stunned look on her roommate's face. "Trish, you look like you're in a trance."

"I just felt someone kiss me on the neck," said Trish, still in shock. "I saw a guy standing at the door, and then he vanished."

"That happened to me last night!" said Marlee.

"Do you think there's any connection between these kisses and the Ouija board?"

"Let's find out."

They set up the Ouija board to talk to HIJ. But he wasn't

in the mood to communicate. Every question they asked, he responded with G-O.

"Go where?" asked Marlee, sounding frustrated.

N-E-C-E-L-L-A-R.

"He wants us to go to the cellar, Trish. Want to sneak down there?"

"It's past curfew, and it's kind of scary to be ghost hunting. But what the heck. Let's go."

Mustering their courage, the girls took a flashlight and headed down the stairs, not knowing what they would find. The cellar had several storage rooms used mostly by the maintenance staff.

"Well, here we are," Trish whispered. "Now what?"

"Let's look for some sign of HIJ."

"I sure hope he's not too ugly, Marlee."

They walked toward the northeast corner, which was part of the original mansion. Here the cellar walls were made of limestone. The flashlight shined on cans of cleaning fluid, rolls of insulation, and pieces of metal pipe.

After 15 minutes of searching, they were about to give up when suddenly Marlee felt a tug on her hair. "What do you want, Trish?"

"Nothing, why?"

"Didn't you just pull on my hair?"

"No."

As her nerves began to quiver, Marlee felt chilled, moist lips press on her left cheek. "Oh, gross!" she yelped, frantically wiping her face. "Another cold, wet kiss!" While Marlee was rubbing her face and holding the flashlight, the beam danced around the unlit room.

"Oh, my gosh!" Trish gasped. "I saw him for just an instant

when the light went by him! Give me the flashlight." Trish shined it around the room.

Suddenly another cold, wet kiss was planted square on her mouth. "Yuck!" Trish sputtered, wiping her lips with the back of her hand. "I just got kissed!"

She was so startled that she dropped the flashlight. It landed on the edge of a bag of cement so that the beam of light was angled up toward the northeast corner of the cellar. When Trish bent down to pick it up, Marlee stopped her roommate's hand from touching it. "Trish! Look at the wall!"

The beam shined on a large heart that had been carved in the soft limestone wall. Scratched inside the heart was HIJ + NAE.

"HIJ? Northeast cellar? Trish, the Ouija was right!"

"I think we'd better leave now," said Trish, her shaky voice revealing her anxiety.

The girls scurried back to their room, relieved they hadn't been caught for breaking curfew, but upset by their eerie experience. They sat on the edge of their beds, silently trying to figure out what had just happened.

"HIJ's ghost kissed us, didn't he, Marlee?"

"Let's find out for sure." Marlee pulled out the Ouija board and asked to talk with HIJ.

"Did you kiss us?" she asked. The indicator didn't move. "Answer me!" she ordered. "Did you kiss us?"

The indicator slowly inched its way toward NO, but then it made a U-turn and zoomed across the board, stopping on YES.

"Aaaaahhhh!" shrieked the girls, their hands covering their faces. "We were kissed by a ghost!"

"What will we do?" Trish asked.

"Demand that he stop." Looking at the Ouija board, Marlee said, "Okay, HIJ, the fun is over. We hate what you've done. You must promise to stop kissing us, okay?"

YES.

"Whew, that's a relief," said Trish.

In a firm voice Marlee told HIJ, "Now please go away and don't ever come back!"

BYE.

"Let's get rid of this board and never use it again," said Trish.

"I agree," Marlee replied, slipping it under her bed. "It won't be soon enough to give it back to Kevin."

A shrill scream from the room across the hall sent both girls leaping to their feet. "That sounds like Toni!" said Trish. "Let's go!"

They rushed into the room where classmate Toni Foggia was pacing back and forth with her arms wrapped around her chest. "It's beyond belief," she claimed, shaking her head. "I was standing here ironing a blouse when out of nowhere I felt someone kiss me on the neck. Except I was all alone. I can't explain it, but I thought I saw a guy standing by the closet door. I blinked, and he was gone."

Trish and Marlee looked at each other in shock.

"I know what you're thinking," said Toni. "But I'm not crazy, and I didn't imagine it. I really felt someone give me a big smooch."

Another bloodcurdling scream pierced the air. "It's coming from Sally and Margie's room!" gasped Marlee. She, Trish, and Toni tore down the hall and burst into the room where Sally Aker stood trembling, her back scrunched against a corner of the room. "You're not going to believe this," she said. "I don't believe it myself. But I had this weird feeling that I was being watched. It was creepy. And then these invisible icy lips kissed me so hard I couldn't move my lips or open my mouth to scream. I kept backing up. When I finally broke free, a boy suddenly appeared, and then, poof, he was gone!"

Sally's roommate, Margie Campbell, appeared in the doorway. Her face was drained of color, and her eyes were so wide her brows disappeared under her bangs.

"Margie!" said Trish. "You look like you're in shock."

"I am. I think I'm sick—sick in the head. I'm imagining things." Margie staggered into the room and slumped in a chair. "I'm going nuts. I was walking up the stairs when I felt a cold, invisible hand brush the bangs off my face. And then I felt someone giving me kisses all over my cheeks. I waved my hands in front of my face and ran up the stairs. What's wrong with me?"

"There's nothing wrong with you," replied Marlee. "You didn't imagine it. Margie, Sally, Toni, you guys better sit down, because what I'm about to say is going to sound really bizarre." They sat down and Marlee continued. "Trish and I are pretty sure we've all been kissed"—she hesitated as she looked squarely in the frightened eyes of each of the girls—"by a ghost!"

Her fellow students didn't scoff. They were still too upset. They listened intently as Trish and Marlee told them about HIJ and how they had contacted him through the Ouija board.

"He promised he wouldn't kiss us anymore," said Marlee. "I believed him, but I guess he lied to us."

Trish snapped her fingers and said, "He promised not to kiss you or me. But he didn't promise not to kiss others."

Marlee slapped her forehead and groaned. "What have we started? I never should have used the Ouija board."

"What's this about a Ouija board?"

"Miss Duncan!"

Looming in the doorway was the school's headmistress, Edna Duncan. She wasn't very happy. "Young ladies, we're on the honor system here. Who has a Ouija board?"

Marlee and Trish reluctantly raised their hands.

Miss Duncan shook her head. "I'm surprised at you two. You know you're not allowed to have one. Where is it?"

The girls led her to their room, where Marlee pulled it out from under her bed.

"Do you know how dangerous these things are?" stated Miss Duncan. "I happen to know something about them. Ouija boards may not have any power of their own, but some people say these boards can tune you in with psychic energy, much like a candle or music or a book can put you in a certain mood."

The girls had no idea that Miss Duncan knew about such things, but she clearly had strong opinions about them.

"I've read cases about ghosts making their presence known only after they've been invited from the spirit world into our own world," said Miss Duncan. "One of the ways that happens is when you are in the right mood to receive them. And then who knows what terrible things might happen."

"I think we found out," muttered Marlee, her eyes downcast.

"What is that supposed to mean?"

Marlee told Mrs. Duncan about the spirit they had contacted. "And now he's going around kissing all of us. Miss Duncan, I'm so sorry!"

Horror spread across the headmistress' face. "Did this ghost give a name?"

"Only initials—HIJ."

"Henry Irving Jacobs!"

"You know him?"

Miss Duncan looked at the doorway where Sally, Margie, and Toni had gathered to eavesdrop. "Young ladies, go to your rooms and stay there," she ordered before closing the door. She then told Trish and Marlee to sit down on their beds while she pulled up a desk chair.

She shook her head and sighed. "You've broken the rules and will have to be punished. Thanks to you, the Kissing Ghost of Rosemont has returned to harass innocent girls."

"Who is the Kissing Ghost?" asked Marlee.

"Henry Irving Jacobs was the son of Charles Jacobs, the caretaker of the Endicott estate long before it became a girls' school. The Jacobs family lived in a cottage off the main house and tended to the upkeep of the grounds and the mansion. Henry was extremely shy and hardly said a word to anyone. No one knew that he had a secret crush on one of the Endicott daughters, Nancy Ann. She was 16 at the time, and he was 15. She was as nice to him as she was toward everyone else. But then she was sent off to boarding school.

"The day before she left, she said her good-byes to the house staff and gave them all kisses. She found Henry in the cellar and gave him a peck on the cheek. He was too shy to kiss her back, but he thought she had strong feelings only for him. After she left he carved a heart in the side of a limestone wall in the cellar and put in his and Nancy's initials."

"We saw the heart with the initials!" Trish said. "They were in the northeast corner of the cellar—right where the spirit said we'd find him."

"Anyway," Miss Duncan continued, "Henry must have been distracted, because while adjusting the furnace in the cellar, he turned a valve the wrong way. A steam pipe exploded and Henry was killed."

"How terrible," said Marlee. "That must have happened in 1928, because the spirit told us that's when he died."

"Please don't interrupt," said Miss Duncan. "When the school opened up years later, no one saw any ghosts. For that matter, no one thought much about them. But then, in 1955, a young student who didn't know any better brought a Ouija board up to her room. She and her roommate were playing with it when a spirit with the initials HIJ began communicating with them. At first they didn't believe he was a spirit. But soon they were getting attacked by a ghost. He would sneak up and give them cold, wet kisses at all hours of the day and night. And then he started smooching the other girls at the academy.

"Eventually the girls figured out it was HIJ—Henry Irving Jacobs. Too shy in life to kiss a girl, he tried to make up for it in death. When given a chance he began kissing every girl in the academy."

"So how did they get rid of him?" Trish asked.

"They used the Ouija board to contact him and made it clear that his kissing attacks were very wrong. They phoned Nancy Ann Endicott, who still lived in the area, and explained the situation. She came over and told Henry that she was very angry at him. If he cared for her at all, he would cease these attacks. The kissing stopped immediately.

"The headmistress made each girl at the academy pledge

never to mention the Kissing Ghost to anyone, and she also banned Ouija boards. She feared that if the Kissing Ghost story were known, at least one curious future student would be foolhardy enough to contact Henry Irving Jacobs, and the kissing attacks would start all over again. Well, she was right. During the following years we didn't have any ghostly kisses—until now."

"We're so very sorry," said Trish. "We didn't know."

"Miss Duncan," asked Marlee, "if it had been a secret, how is it you know so much about the Kissing Ghost?"

The headmistress remained silent for a long time before she confessed, "Because back in 1955, I was the Rosemont student whose Ouija board was responsible for the kissing attacks."

The girls of Rosemont Academy were sworn to secrecy about mentioning the Kissing Ghost to anyone else.

Meanwhile Miss Duncan, Marlee, and Trish sat down with the Ouija board and called up Henry Irving Jacobs's spirit. In no uncertain terms, Miss Duncan scolded Henry, ordered him to leave, and reminded him that Nancy would be very upset to learn he was harassing students again.

When the session was finished, Miss Duncan took away the Ouija board and told Marlee and Trish, "I'm afraid that I'll have to ground both of you for breaking the rules. You cannot have visitors or leave the academy for the next 30 days."

"I accept the punishment, Miss Duncan," said Trish.

"Me too," Marlee added. "I promise not to touch a Ouija board again. The only guy I want kissing me is a living one— like Robby Cooper. But I guess there's no chance of that happening, at least not for another month."

SCREAMS OF HORROR, CRIES OF TERROR

"Night after night the terror-stricken villagers peeked out their windows and waited. Would the headless ghoul stagger down the streets again as he had every midnight for a petrifying week? Would he again send dogs howling in fright? Force men to cower? Provoke nightmares in children?

"As the clock struck midnight, a scream shattered the dark calm, echoing down the cobblestone street. Doors and shutters slammed shut. Torches were doused.

"The ghoul, the horrible headless ghoul, had returned! Step by staggering step, the body lurched from one doorway to another in search of . . . what?

"The fiend stopped at a cottage and groped for the door. On the other side young Timmy Landis braced himself against the weathered door, knowing full well the broken lock would not hold. The ghoul lowered his shoulder and splintered the wood, sending Timmy sprawling across the room. Timmy lay helplessly on the floor as the headless horror advanced closer and closer—"

RIIINNNGGG . . . RIIINNNGGG.

"Oh, darn, that's the bell, kids," clucked librarian Elaine Lundgren as she closed the big black book. "I'll continue reading the story on Wednesday."

"Not fair!" declared one of the 20 fifth-grade students who had been sitting in rapt attention on the floor of Packer School's media center.

"You can't stop now," complained another listener. "What happened to Timmy?"

"You must be patient," Mrs. Lundgren said sweetly. "You're scheduled to be back in the media center in two days." She carefully placed the book behind her desk on a special shelf reserved for only the most important books. "The school buses are waiting. I don't want you to miss your rides."

Reluctantly the students got up and headed for their classroom to collect their things. But one boy, Joshua Coleman, stayed behind. *I've got to find out what happens,* he thought. *I can't wait until Wednesday. I know—I'll sneak the book home and then bring it back in the morning before class. She won't know it's gone. It's not like it's stealing or anything. I'm just borrowing it.*

To help cover up this "unauthorized loan," Joshua walked over to another shelf and found a book about the same size and color as the horror book that Mrs. Lundgren had been reading aloud. When no one was looking, he switched copies and quickly stuffed the spooky book under his sweater. Then he scooted out the door and into his classroom. Crouching in a corner with his back to the other kids, he pulled out the book and put it in his backpack before catching the bus.

On the way home Emily Rosewood, who was sitting behind Joshua, told other riders who were in earshot, "You won't believe what happened to me at the media center today. I was trying to find a poem about Halloween. I looked everywhere, in poetry books and stuff about Halloween, but I couldn't find a single poem. So I had just about given up when I tripped over a book on the floor that I hadn't noticed before. I went to pick it up and—here's where it gets real creepy—it was opened to a page with a poem about Halloween!"

"Yeah, right," sneered Joshua.

"No, really, it's true," Emily insisted.

"Ooh, how weird," added Sally Mahon from across the aisle.

"Emily, now that you mention it, I had a strange thing happen to me last year when I was searching in the media center's computer," declared Mike Coburn, a sixth grader who was sitting next to Joshua. "I wanted to look up stuff on motocross racing, but I struck out. I started to walk away when the computer began typing out things on its own. I mean, I didn't even touch the keys or anything. And the computer flashed the title of a new book about sports. I found it, and sure enough there was a whole chapter about motocross."

"Maybe the media center has a friendly ghost," offered Sally.

"Maybe you're all creeped out because this is Halloween week," Joshua said. Then he added sarcastically, "The next thing you'll be telling us is the bogeyman leaped out of the B shelf, and a goblin came out of the G shelf."

The kids laughed. "Of all the places to haunt," Joshua continued, "you'd think a ghost would pick a place more scary than a library."

The book that Joshua had swiped was titled *Screams of Horror, Cries of Terror.* Bound in smooth, shiny black leather with gold lettering in old English type on the cover, the oversize book looked brand new. No creases on the spine, no bent edges, no torn or folded pages.

The book, a collection of short horror stories, was handwritten by Gertrude Wickham, the former librarian at Packer Elementary. Tall and bony, Miss Wickham could pass for the good twin of the wicked witch in *The Wizard of Oz.* Her long, pointed nose and her frizzy shoulder-length gray hair only enhanced the image. It didn't help matters that, without looking, kids could always tell when Miss Wickham was heading their way. The joints in her knees and ankles creaked whenever she walked or got up from her chair.

Despite her physical features, she displayed a warm smile that appealed to kids, hazel eyes that brimmed with understanding, and a soft voice that brought comfort to young students who felt lost in a library.

Miss Wickham loved books and tried to share her enthusiasm with students. She encouraged them to read whatever interested them—biographies, sports, mysteries, ghost stories. "Reading," she would always say, "exercises the muscles of the mind."

Miss Wickham tried to get kids excited about books by reading stories aloud to them. Every year around Halloween it became a tradition to read spooky tales and recite scary poems that often caused her attentive listeners to experience a slight case of the willies.

The library—she refused to call it a media center—at Packer Elementary was her life. She lived alone and had few outside interests other than students and books. Miss Wickham lovingly straightened up the books, making sure each one was in its proper place: spine out, fiction in alphabetical order by author, nonfiction by category. She didn't mind if the kids talked as long as they spoke in hushed tones. She wanted the library to be a friendly place.

For reasons that no one could figure out, Miss Wickham never shared the book she had written with anyone. In fact, no one knew the book even existed or that she could write. Until that fateful day.

Late one afternoon at a table in the back of the library, Miss Wickham was slouched in a chair, her head down and arms dangling limply by her side. An open book lay on her lap. At first Oscar the janitor thought she was sleeping. But when he nudged her, she began to tip over. Oscar managed to catch her, and when he did, he felt her cold skin. That's when he knew Miss Wickham was dead. She was 73 years old.

After the body was removed, assistant librarian Elaine Lundgren examined the book that Miss Wickham had been reading—*Screams of Horror, Cries of Terror.* Only when she glanced at the byline did she discover that its author was none other than Gertrude Wickham herself.

Mrs. Lundgren took the book home and read it from cover to cover. Written in flawless penmanship with a blue fountain pen, the book contained two dozen horror stories on 212 crisp white pages. It seemed odd that such delicate, flowing handwriting would form words about such bone-chilling subjects as screaming skulls, headless ghouls, and bloodthirsty monsters. Some stories were too intense for the lower grades. But other tales were quite good and worthy of being read to classes.

Mrs. Lundgren, who took over as head media specialist, decided that the book would be kept on the shelf with other books that only teachers could use. Students knew they were not allowed to touch them, and under no circumstances were the books—especially *Screams of Horror, Cries of Terror*—to leave the school library.

Joshua understood the library rules, but he simply had to find out Timmy's fate.

When Joshua arrived home he dropped his backpack and went outside to play. After dinner he did his homework and watched television until it was time for bed. He kissed his parents good night, snuck a soda out of the refrigerator, and headed off to his room without the usual nighttime begging for an extra half hour of television.

As he sat on his bed he put the book in his lap and thumbed through the pages to find the story "Revenge of the Headless Ghoul." *Ah, here it is,* he told himself. *Now I can find out what happened to Timmy.* He began reading.

Frozen in fear Timmy lay on the floor as the headless horror swayed closer and closer. Timmy tried to utter a cry for help, but only silence left his lips. The monster stood over the terrified youngster, whose heart was pounding so rapidly he was on the brink of swooning. The ghoul bent over, and his massive, gnarled fingers slowly reached for Timmy's throat.

Joshua stopped reading because he became aware of a very uncomfortable sensation—an icy feeling and a slight pressure around his neck. He shuddered, furiously rubbed his neck, and cleared his throat with a couple of coughs. He clutched his can of soda and began guzzling it when an unexpected and tremendously loud clap of thunder shook the house. Already skittish about the monster, the startled boy spilled his soda all over the final two pages of the story.

"Oh, no!" he moaned. The liquid spread over the adjoining pages and then collected in the binding. Joshua quickly picked up the book and tilted it, letting the soda run off onto the floor. Then he ran into the bathroom and returned with a towel to soak up the remaining soda on the pages. He rubbed hard—too hard. He wiped off the liquid, but to his shock he discovered that he had smeared the words on the two pages. The soda had mixed with the ink to turn the words into blotches of blues and browns. Fortunately, no other pages were damaged, but that didn't make Joshua feel any better.

He grabbed his hair and stomped around his room. *I don't believe what I just did! I'm going to be in so much trouble, they'll probably kick me out of school! What can I do? Oh, why did I bring this dumb book home!*

Afraid and ashamed to tell his parents, Joshua lay in bed for hours, staring at the ceiling and fretting. Eventually he nodded off.

Long before dawn Joshua was stirred awake by a cracking sound, like the snapping of a person's ankle or knee joints. "Mom? Dad? Is that you?" he asked.

There was no reply other than an occasional snap or crack. *Someone is in the room! Do something! Flip on the light. No, stay perfectly still, and maybe he'll go away. Or should I make a run for the door? Or grab my baseball bat? What should I do?*

The boy's eyes focused on the far end of the room. *Oh, no! Someone is here! A burglar! Or a murderer! I can't lie here and wait to be killed.* Shaking so badly he was afraid the bed would move and make a noise, Joshua ever so slowly reached down and snared the baseball bat he kept under his bed. Then, in one swift motion, he flipped on the bedside light, jumped to his feet while still on the bed, and cocked his arms, ready to swing his bat.

Across the room stood a tall woman, her face framed by long gray hair under a black hooded cloak that smelled like it had been kept in a musty closet for too many years.

"Aaahhh!" Joshua shouted. "A witch!"

She held out a bony arm and pointed toward the boy. "For shame! For shame!" she hissed. "What you did is wrong, so very wrong!"

"What are you talking about?"

"Don't play games with me. You know. You've shown no respect for the rules—rules put in place to avoid the kinds of mindless behavior that ruins it for everyone. Now do what's right. Confess your misdeed and accept your punishment."

She whipped the cloak tightly around her body. Then she turned and stalked toward the door, her knees and ankles snapping with each step. When she reached the door the intruder didn't bother opening it. Instead, to Joshua's utter amazement, she walked right through the door!

Having heard Joshua talking, his parents entered the room and gawked at their son, who was still standing on the bed with a bat on his shoulder.

"What in the world are you doing playing baseball on your bed at this hour?" asked his baffled mother.

Joshua sheepishly put down the bat and stepped off the bed. He was so shook up he couldn't speak. How was he going to explain this when he himself didn't understand what had happened?

Finally he said, "Um, I know this is going to sound crazy

70

. . . but would you believe me if I told you a witch was in my room—"

"Not likely," said his father between yawns.

"—and that she scolded me and then walked through my bedroom door without opening it?"

In a tone that made it clear she was trying to humor Joshua, his mother asked, "What did she say?"

"She said that what I did was wrong, and that I should admit it."

"What is it you did?"

"Nothing. I was sleeping, and then this witch appears."

"Tell me, Josh," said his father, "did you do something yesterday that, upon reflection, you might feel was wrong?"

Joshua decided to confess—but only partly. "Well, um, I did borrow a book without permission from the media center that wasn't supposed to leave the school. But, honest, I was going to bring it back first thing this morning." He pointed to the book on the beside table.

His mother picked it up, glanced at the cover and said, "*Screams of Horror, Cries of Terror.* Looks like a scary book. Were you reading it tonight?"

"Yes."

"It seems to me that you had a nightmare because you were reading a horror story. And the witch said those things because you're feeling guilty about sneaking the book out of the school when you knew better."

"You're probably right, Mom." Joshua sighed. "But she sure seemed real."

"Let's get some sleep," she said. "It's almost 3:30. Later this morning when you arrive at school, I trust you'll do the right thing."

"Yes, Mom," muttered Joshua.

"A nightmare can sometimes be your conscience trying to teach you a lesson," added his father.

If it really was a nightmare, Joshua thought.

That morning Joshua arrived at the media center before the first bell rang and was relieved not to see Mrs. Lundgren at her desk. He pulled the book out of his backpack and was just about to put it back on the shelf when he heard Mrs. Lundgren ask, "What were you doing, Joshua?"

"I was, um . . ." He opened the book at random to a page that featured a pen-and-ink drawing. *A woman in a hooded cloak, long hair, pointy nose, and bulging eyes! That's the witch who was in my room last night!* He stared at the picture and shuddered.

"Well, Joshua?"

His mind swirled with dreadful thoughts. The witch. Mrs. Lundgren. Caught red-handed. "I was, um, just thumbing through the book *Screams of Horror, Cries of Terror,* and I saw this drawing of a witch."

"Oh, yes, the witch. Do you know who that is?"

"No."

"That's Miss Wickham, the librarian who wrote the book. You wouldn't have known her because this is your first year at Packer. She died less than two years ago. She wasn't really as frightening as that drawing. She had a friend do the illustrations for the book, and Miss Wickham posed for this drawing by dressing up like a witch. She teased her hair and gave a frightful scowl."

Mrs. Lundgren looked off into the distance and sighed. "Miss Wickham was a dedicated librarian. I miss her. But sometimes I get the feeling she's still around."

Mrs. Lundgren took the book away from Joshua and put it on the shelf. "You really shouldn't be back here, Joshua. You know that these books—especially this one—are to be handled only by the staff."

"I'm sorry, Mrs. Lundgren. I'd better get to class now."

"What's this?" she asked, closely examining the spine. "It looks like a water mark. Joshua, do you know anything about this?"

"No, ma'am," he fibbed.

He held his breath as he watched her thumb through a few pages. He exhaled when she put the book away. *Wow, was that a close call. I got away with it! I'm home free!*

Heading toward the entrance, he walked down an aisle between two shelves when a book mysteriously fell off. It conked him square on the head, bounced off his shoulder, and landed open-faced on the floor.

"Ouch," he said. He looked around and noticed that only he and Mrs. Lundgren, who was at her desk on the other side of the room, were in the media center. *The book fell all by itself!* he thought. He picked it up. *Hey, it's* Pinocchio. *I like that story.* He began reading the page where the book had opened:

After telling the third lie, Pinocchio's nose grew so long that he couldn't turn around. If he turned one way, he struck it against the bedpost or the window. If he turned the other, he hit the wall or the door. The Fairy looked at him and began to laugh.

"Why are you laughing?" asked the marionette sheepishly.

"I laugh at the foolish lies you have told."

"How did you know they were lies?"

"Lies, my boy, are recognized at once, because they are of only two kinds. Some have short legs, and others have long noses. Yours are the kind that have long noses."

Pinocchio was so crestfallen that he tried to run away and hide himself, but he couldn't. His nose had grown so long that he couldn't get it through the door.

The Fairy let the marionette cry and howl for a good half hour on account of his long nose. She did this in order to teach him a lesson upon the folly of telling falsehoods.

Joshua had read enough. He closed the book, put it back on the shelf, took a deep breath, and approached the librarian. "Mrs. Lundgren, I have something to tell you. You know that story you were reading to us yesterday about the headless man? Well, I couldn't wait until Wednesday to find out how it ended, so I took the book home with me. I started to read it in my bedroom, and I accidentally spilled soda on it. When I tried to wipe it up, I smeared the last two pages of the story, and, well, gee"—his eyes started clouding up with tears—"I'm so sorry, Mrs. Lundgren."

The librarian turned pale and pulled out the book. She flipped through it until she came to the blotted pages. "Oh, my dear! Oh, no! This is terrible! The pages are absolutely ruined!"

She pursed her lips and frowned. "Joshua, I'm upset and very disappointed. You know you aren't supposed to take this book out of the library. It's very special, one-of-a-kind. Yet you deliberately broke one of our rules, and now look what happened. Two pages are ruined." She tried hard to control her anger. "I'm glad you came forward and told the truth. That's very important. But, still, you must face the consequences."

"What are they?"

"For starters, a trip to the principal's office. Let's go."

As they walked out of the media center, Mrs. Lundgren told Joshua, "Miss Wickham wouldn't have tolerated such a violation of the rules. As sweet and nice as she was, she would erupt like a volcano if anyone took a reference book out of the library.

"The worst thing a student could do was steal a book. Her eyes would blaze, and she would deliver a tongue-lashing that left kids shaking in their socks. Steal a book? That was like someone kidnapping her child, not that she had one, mind you. But to ruin two pages? My goodness, Joshua, Miss Wickham would have scared you silly."

Still reeling from the image of his nighttime visitor, he said, "Mrs. Lundgren, I think she already did." At that moment he knew who—or rather, what—had knocked the book *Pinocchio* off the shelf.

For his punishment Joshua had to spend a month during recess in the media center, erasing pencil marks from books. The worst part was that he never learned the ending to "The Revenge of the Headless Ghoul." But once he began using the library with newfound respect, he was never haunted again.

THE PHANTOM GRADUATE

"**T**he day is finally here," Brooke Mason declared. "All those years in classrooms, and now in a matter of hours it will all be over. We'll be high school graduates!"

She took her right hand off the steering wheel of her car and reached over to her boyfriend, Kip Nielsen. He squeezed her hand and replied, "This is awesome. We're free at last—at least for the next three months until we go off to college."

Brooke groaned. "Then we'll start the whole process all over again."

The two seniors were heading to graduation ceremonies at Adams High School. More than 400 students were slated to receive their diplomas.

"No more listening to those boring lectures in English literature from Mrs. Williams," Kip proclaimed.

"No more snide remarks from Mr. Thomas, making fun of the clothes we wear," added Brooke.

"No more eating what the cafeteria calls lunch."

"No more first-period gym class."

"No more . . . Brooke, look out!"

A teenage girl wearing a white mortar cap and gown and a gold and blue stole was crossing the street directly in front of their car. Brooke slammed on the brakes. The girl stopped in her tracks and, with a horrified look on her face, held out her hands, waiting for the impact. Fortunately the car screeched to a halt only a few inches from the girl. She then returned to the curb.

"She walked right out in front of us," said Brooke, still shaking from the near-miss. "I didn't even see her step off the curb."

"I didn't either," Kip said. "She came out of nowhere." He rolled down the window and called out to the girl, "Are you all right?"

Adjusting her cap the girl replied, "Yes, I'm fine. I'm sorry. It was all my fault. I hope I didn't give you too much of a scare."

"Once our nerves calm down we'll be okay," he said. "You could have been killed."

"I'm sorry, I wasn't paying attention. I had a serious problem with my car, and I need to get to the graduation ceremonies."

"Adams High?" asked Kip. After she nodded he said, "Well, hop in, and we'll give you a lift. We're heading there too."

"Thanks." As she slipped into the backseat, she examined the interior and the dashboard with admiration. "Wow, what a fancy car. What is it?"

"It's not so fancy," Brooke replied. "It's a 1989 Acura Integra."

"I never heard of it."

"Oh, sure, they've been around since the mid-1980s," said Kip.

"Oh, no wonder," she murmured.

That's an odd remark, thought Kip. But neither he nor Brooke bothered to question the passenger about it. "I'm Kip Nielsen and this, the driver you darn near scared to death, is Brooke Mason."

"Hi, I'm Laurie Russo. Again, I'm sorry. I was in such a hurry because I didn't want to miss graduation. I've been waiting a long, long time for this moment. And I don't want to blow it again."

"Again?" asked Brooke.

"Oh, nothing," replied Laurie. "It's a long story."

Brooke looked in the rearview mirror at Laurie. *I don't recognize her. But I don't know everybody in school, it's so big.* Brooke kept glancing between the road and the rearview mirror, studying the girl's features. Her big, brown eyes and lush eyebrows dominated her slender face, which was framed by thick, curly shoulder-length black hair.

"I see you're wearing a gold and blue stole," said Kip.

"Yes," said Laurie, "it's for the National Honor Society."

"Congratulations. I guess Brooke and I spent too much time goofing off and not enough studying, or else we might have made it into the National Honor Society."

"I know it's a big school, Laurie, but I don't remember seeing you," said Brooke. "Did you go all four years to Adams?"

"Yes."

"Do you belong to any clubs or organizations?"

"Glee Club."

"I thought that disbanded a few years ago."

"No," said Laurie. "Don't you remember when we sang cuts from Michael Jackson's album *Thriller* on Seniors Day?"

Brooke and Kip looked at each other. "Uh, no," he replied. "The only group playing that day was the Trash Compactors."

"I don't know them," said Laurie. "So, are you guys college-bound?"

"Yes," replied Brooke. "I'm going to Central Michigan, and Kip is going to Michigan State. What about you?"

Laurie pulled out an envelope from under her gown, opened it, and held up a letter. "I'm holding a dream come true in my hand. It's from the Student Ambassador's Program. 'Dear Laurie Russo,'" she read from the letter. "'We are pleased to inform you that you have been selected to be a Student Ambassador, representing the United States in Italy from June 15 through August 15. Upon the successful completion of your duties as a Student Ambassador, you will be allowed to enroll in studies at the University of Rome under full scholarship.'"

She put down the letter. "I won't bore you with all the other details, but it's going to be so exciting!"

"Wow, that's pretty cool," said Brooke. "You must be excited."

"Imagine, studying in Rome and having my tuition, books, room and board all paid for. This letter is the most important possession I own. It goes everywhere with me."

"Maybe you should ask Mr. Banducci for some tips on living in Rome," Brooke suggested. "He's from Italy, you know."

"Who's Mr. Banducci?" asked Laurie.

"Laurie, he's our assistant principal. You must know that."

"But I thought . . . oh, never mind."

Kip winked at Brooke and joked, "Laurie must have spent all her time studying and staying out of trouble, so she never had to meet Mr. Banducci."

"Well, here we are," Brooke announced as she steered the car into the school parking lot. "We're about to walk into the Adams High gym for the last time."

"All right!" Kip exclaimed.

"It means a lot for me to make it to this ceremony," said Laurie. "It's been a long time in coming."

"Yes," Brooke agreed, "twelve years of school."

"Thanks for the lift. You'll never know how important it was for me to be here."

"Hey, no problem," Brooke responded. "Glad to help. But promise to look both ways before crossing the street!"

"Especially in Rome," added Kip.

"Okay, ladies and gentlemen," said Vice Principal Banducci over the loudspeaker. "Let's get ready to graduate!" Cheers erupted from inside the home rooms of the senior class. "You all know what to do. Line up in alphabetical order in the hallways, and a teacher will lead you into the gym, where the processional will get underway. Once you get to your chair, remain standing until you see Miss Walters give you the signal to sit down. When it's time for the passing out of diplomas, each row will take its turn. You'll walk up to the side of the stage behind the curtain and then wait for your name to be called. Miss Walters will tell you when it's your row's turn. Good luck and congratulations!"

Toward the back of a hallway, the students whose last names began with R lined up. Dara Runnels and Katie Rutter were puzzled when an unfamiliar black-haired girl asked their names and then slipped in line between them. During rehearsal, Dara and Katie had been next to each other, according to the alphabet.

"Pardon me," said Dara, "but are you sure you're in the right place?"

"You're Runnels and she's Rutter. I'm Russo. So I should be between you two."

Dara shrugged and muttered, "I guess so."

Members of the graduating class headed down the hallways and streamed into the gym while a tape blared the song "Pomp and Circumstance." They filed into their assigned rows of folding chairs on the gym floor. Everything was going smoothly until the *R*'s were filling their rows. Dara stood in front of the last seat in one row while Katie and the rest of the R's entered the next row. But Laurie, looking confused, stood by Dara's side.

"Oh, dear, what is going on?" fretted the busy Miss Walters, who had many other things on her mind.

Laurie whispered anxiously, "I don't have a chair."

"I thought everyone knew where they were supposed to go. What's your name?"

"Russo, Laurie Russo."

"I can't recall the name, but since you follow Dara, you should be the first one in the next row." Realizing that the next row was already filled, the annoyed teacher ordered, "Wait right here." Miss Walters scurried off and returned with a folding chair. Then she walked away, muttering, "There's one in every crowd."

Once all the graduates had assembled, Miss Walters gave the signal for them to sit down. As the school officials were introduced up on stage, Laurie whispered to Dara, "Where's Mrs. Fitzgerald?"

"Who?"

"Mrs. Fitzgerald, our principal."

"She retired three years ago." Dara stared at Laurie and thought, *I know just about everybody in school, but I don't remember her.*

Laurie kept glancing up at the bleachers. "I wish I could find my parents," she told Dara. "They were hoping to get a good seat. They're so proud of me. I'll be the first one in the family to graduate high school. My parents never finished high school. They came over from Italy in 1965 and started a bakery."

"Shhh, I think Kim Soto is about to give her valedictorian speech."

"But I thought Jimmy Unger was our valedictorian."

"Never heard of him. Are you sure you're in the right school?" Dara asked half in jest.

Finally it was time to pass out the diplomas. "Oh, this is getting so exciting," squealed Laurie. "I can't wait." Dara noticed that Laurie was literally squirming in her seat with anticipation as she waited for their row to be called. Finally Miss Walters signaled to them. "This is it!" beamed Laurie.

The students stood up, walked to the side aisle, climbed the stairs to the stage, and waited for their name to be called: "Michael Thomas Roberts . . . Peri Nicole Roland . . . Kelly Suzanne Roper . . . Phillip David Rowen . . . Dara Theresa Runnels . . ."

"Congratulations, Dara," whispered Laurie.

"Thanks," Dara replied without looking back as she marched out with a big smile.

". . . Katie Margaret Rutter . . ."

After accepting her diploma, Dara glanced behind her and saw Katie, not Laurie, walking behind her. When Dara returned to her seat, she looked around for Laurie. *They didn't call Laurie's name. I wonder what happened. She seemed like she couldn't wait to get her diploma. And now she's not here. That's so weird.*

When the ceremony ended and the class gave one final cheer, the students marched out of the gym and onto the school grounds where they kissed, hugged, and patted each other on the back.

While offering congratulations and good luck to her fellow students, Dara found Katie. "I'm glad I caught up with you, Katie. What happened to that girl, Laurie Russo? She was right behind me. But when I went up to get my diploma, they called your name next, not hers. And she never returned to her seat."

"I didn't even notice," said Katie. "I led the next row. When I got up on the side of the stage, waiting to be called, I was making sure my cap was on right. I remember hearing your name and seeing you walk up to get your diploma. And then they called my name."

"But you must have seen Laurie right behind me when we reached the stage. She whispered congratulations to me just before my name was called."

"It's pretty hard to tell you two apart from behind, especially in a cap and gown. You're both about the same height and build and have shoulder-length black hair. I assumed Laurie was in front of me. But it was you."

"So what happened to Laurie?"

"We did it! We did it!" Kip rejoiced as he picked Brooke up by the waist and twirled her around. "We are now officially high school graduates!"

He opened the door to her car and placed his camera in

the backseat when he noticed an envelope on the floor. "What's this?" He opened it and pulled out a letter. "It's from the Students Ambassador Program and addressed to Laurie Russo. She must have left it in the car."

"Oh, Kip, remember she said it was the most important letter of her life? We should return it to her."

"We're not going to find her in this crowd. Her address is on this letter, 233-B Holman Avenue. Let's drop it off after we have dinner with our parents at the restaurant."

After they got into the car, Brooke said, "I find Laurie very odd, but I can't put my finger on why."

"Besides the fact that neither one of us remembers seeing her before? And that she talked about the Glee Club we don't have?"

"Yes, and she didn't know who Mr. Banducci was or that the Trash Compactors played on Seniors Day."

The couple brushed off further suspicion while enjoying a hearty meal at the restaurant with their parents. As they were about to leave, Brooke and Kip bumped into Dara, who invited them to a graduation party. "We'll be over shortly," said Brooke. "We have a letter to drop off at someone's house. By the way, do you know a girl named Laurie Russo?"

"Well, sort of."

"Brooke almost killed her this afternoon—although it wasn't Brooke's fault," said Kip. He then told Dara how they met Laurie and ended up with her cherished letter.

"She's weird," said Dara, who described her encounter with Laurie at the graduation ceremony. "If you see her, ask her what happened to her. I'm very curious."

"We'll tell you at the party," said Kip. "Bye."

After a ten-minute drive Brooke eased the car next to the curb of a two-story brick duplex. "This is the place, 233-B Holman," said Kip. "It's the upstairs unit."

Answering the door was a short, squat man in his early sixties with curly salt-and-pepper hair ringing an otherwise bald head. He was wearing a white sleeveless T-shirt and baggy black pants.

"Are you Mr. Russo?" Kip asked.

"Yes, what can I do for you?" he asked in a thick Italian accent.

"I have something for Laurie," replied Kip, holding up the envelope. "She left it in our car today."

Mr. Russo winced, turned his head to the side, put a clenched fist to his mouth, and bit his knuckle. He stayed in that position for several seconds.

"Mr. Russo, are you all right?" Brooke asked worriedly.

"Why would you come here today of all days and mention Laurie to me?" the man complained.

"Sir? I don't understand," said Kip, taken aback by Mr. Russo's anger. "Laurie said she had car problems, and we gave her a lift to graduation ceremonies—"

"What?" Mr. Russo asked in disbelief as tears welled up in his eyes. "What?"

From the next room a woman's voice shouted, "Tony, who's at the door?"

"Two kids who said they saw Laurie—today!"

She uttered a heartrending cry and came running to the door. She was a short, rotund gray-haired woman in her late fifties. Her eyes were red from crying. Confronting the teens, she asked, "Are you sure you saw Laurie today?"

"I don't know what's going on here, Mr. and Mrs. Russo,"

said a flustered Kip. "All we want to do is to return this letter to Laurie."

Mr. Russo accepted the envelope, opened it up, and read the first sentence. Then he broke down in gut-wrenching sobs as he handed it to his wife. She took one look, shrieked, and began wailing too.

Bewildered by this unexpected emotional scene, Kip and Brooke stepped back. "Well, um, we'll be leaving now," he said.

"No, wait," said Mr. Russo, reaching out and clutching Kip by the wrist. "You must come in. Tell us everything about Laurie."

Reluctantly Brooke and Kip went inside and recalled their meeting with Laurie as the Russos pumped them for every detail. Her parents seemed to hang on every word as if the two grads were making an immensely important announcement. When the teens finished their account, Kip asked the Russos, "Forgive me for saying this, but the way you're behaving, I get the impression that something has happened to Laurie."

Mrs. Russo started crying again. When she recovered, she said, "You're right." She took a deep breath and said, "Laurie is dead."

"Oh, no!" Brooke blurted out. "How?"

"In a car wreck," Mrs. Russo tearfully replied.

"When did it happen?"

"On this very day, Wednesday, June 1." Mrs. Russo paused before adding, "1983."

"1983?" said Brooke. "You mean—"

"I mean 1983."

"Whoa," said Kip, throwing up his hands. "Brooke, I think you and I better be going."

"Before you go, come with me," said Mr. Russo. They followed him and his wife into another room. On the wall was an 8" x 10" (20cm x 25cm) color photo of a pretty raven-haired girl. Black crepe had been wrapped around the frame, and a small candle flickered on a table beneath the photo.

"That's Laurie!" declared Brooke.

"Yes," said Mr. Russo, "that's our only child, Laurie Marie Russo. On this day 11 years ago she had taken our car because she had to be at graduation early. Our friends, the Zammutos, were going to drive us there later.

"Laurie had on her cap and gown and her National Honor Society stole. She looked so beautiful, so proud. We were bursting with pride. The first Russo in the family to graduate high school. She was going to be a student ambassador in Italy and study at the University of Rome."

Mr. Russo's voice cracked, so his wife picked up the story. "Laurie's car was entering the intersection when a drunk driver roared through the red light and broadsided her. Her car flipped over three times. She died instantly of massive injuries. To this day I can't even go anywhere near the corner of Fifth and Main Street."

"Is that where the accident happened?" asked Kip. The Russos nodded. Turning to Brooke, he said, "That's where we picked her up today!"

Brooke clutched his hand. "Kip," she gasped. "We gave a ride to a ghost!"

The two teens sat motionless, overwhelmed by the news. "No wonder she didn't know who the principal was and talked about the Glee Club that doesn't exist anymore," said Kip. "She was still thinking in terms of 1983. And that's why we didn't know her. She wasn't in our class."

After collecting her thoughts, Brooke said, "I feel sorry for Laurie because she never graduated."

"Oh, but she did," said Mrs. Russo. "See on the other wall? That's her diploma. The school gave it to us after she died. But we never found the letter of acceptance from the Student Ambassador's Program that she kept with her—until now. It breaks my heart to see this letter. Laurie worked so hard to earn it."

"She couldn't wait to graduate," said Mr. Russo. "She looked forward to all the hoopla, the caps and gowns, the marching into the gym, the music. Tell me, kids, did you see Laurie at the graduation ceremonies?"

"Oh, I almost forgot," replied Brooke. "Dara Runnels, a friend of ours, said that Laurie was there. She was in the processional, right behind Dara. Laurie even made it all the way up to side of the stage. But after Dara's name was called, Laurie vanished."

"Why would her ghost appear now, 11 years after she died?" Mrs. Russo wondered.

Mr. Russo turned to his wife, and with a tearful smile, said, "Don't you see what happened? Laurie died on a Wednesday. This is the first June 1 that fell on a Wednesday since her death. Everything had to be just as it was before. Laurie finally got to attend what she had so looked forward to—her high school graduation ceremony."

THE CURSE ON MISSY GREEN

Brynn Slater didn't know what she was hearing at first. The noise sounded wretched and scary, like nothing she had ever heard before.

It began as a low, one-tone moan that soon grew in pitch until it jangled the 12-year-old's nerves. It was so unusual she couldn't tell if it was coming from a human, animal, or machine.

Is the school furnace acting up again? she wondered. *No, that's not it. It sounds more like a living thing. An animal maybe?* She scanned the empty classroom and then gazed out the window, but couldn't find the source.

The eerie sound caused Brynn to wince as it turned into a steady, woeful groan. Brynn stepped out into the hallway, hoping an adult was there who might pinpoint the noise. But the teachers were still in their meeting, and the parents weren't due for another 45 minutes.

Brynn warily went back into the room and finished tacking up the poems that she and her classmates had composed for the parents' open house at Bloom Middle School. Brynn had volunteered to help her seventh-grade teacher, Miss Meyers, get ready for the event.

I wish I hadn't volunteered, she told herself. *I only did it to get a few brownie points. I hate this room. It gives me the creeps.*

The classroom was one of 14 that made up the original school that was built in 1936 in Spalding, Ohio. Although it had modern equipment, including a computer and VCR and fairly new desks, the room itself showed its age: two old pipes running across the high ceiling; big drafty windows; walls painted a dirty yellow; a dark-stained creaky wood floor. The school had a new wing built about 10 years ago that added 20 classrooms. But Brynn was unlucky enough to get placed in a class in the older section.

Brynn nervously glanced at the clock. *It's 6:45. The teachers' meeting should be breaking up any minute now.* Then the frightening sound erupted into a teeth-rattling bellow— seemingly from the depths of a horrid, unknown world—and ended in a mournful wail of unspeakable suffering.

Brynn could no longer take it. Slamming the palms of her hands over her ears, she bolted out of the room and dashed into the teachers' lounge.

"I'm sorry for bursting in here," she said breathlessly. "But there's an awful noise coming from Room 106. Like somebody is dying!"

The teachers streamed out of the lounge and hurried into the classroom. They stopped to listen, but heard only their own breathing.

"I heard this terrible sound," Brynn insisted. "Moaning and groaning. Just awful."

"Well, whatever it was, it's gone," said Miss Meyers. "Maybe it was a cat fight outside. Cats can make very strange, scary sounds when they're fighting."

"I think kids were pulling a prank on you," stated Mr. Gordon, the principal.

Brynn nodded, wanting desperately to believe that's all it was. But in her heart she suspected the source was far more menacing.

She would soon discover how chillingly right she was.

Brynn didn't sleep too well that night, because she kept thinking about that hideous sound. Like an unstoppable tape cassette, the dreadful noise seemed to play over and over in her head. *Why was I the only one who heard it? Oh, I made such a fool of myself. The way all the teachers looked at me, they must think I'm a goofball. And Miss Meyers probably won't call on me ever again in class. I blew it. I royally blew it. What a way to start the year in a new school.*

Brynn had attended Bloom School only a few weeks, having moved from Chicago with her mother after the divorce. They settled in the small town of Spalding because her mom wanted to get away from the big city and start a new life. Spalding fit the bill—a nice, quaint place where her mother found a nursing position.

Although Brynn faced considerable adjustments, she was managing to handle the dramatic changes in her life. She liked Miss Meyers and the kids in her class, but Brynn couldn't shake the uneasy feeling she had about the school itself. Her mother assured her it was normal to react that way about a new school. Brynn wasn't so sure. This feeling was different— so peculiar, in fact, that she couldn't even describe it.

Naturally the groaning incident only intensified her uneasiness. But when weeks went by without a repeat of the noise—which no one else had heard—Brynn assumed it had been the sound of a cat fight or a prank.

However, this belief was dashed one early afternoon after she skipped lunch and decided to stay in the classroom alone to study for an upcoming math test she had forgotten about. While working on practice problems, Brynn became aware of a low growl that quickly turned into an appalling, pain-racked moan.

Brynn dropped her pencil and looked around. *Oh, no, not again,* she thought. *Get out of here, Brynn.* But she couldn't move. Rooted to her seat, Brynn broke out in a sweat, her mind and body paralyzed from fear. The mournful moaning turned into a screech—then a shrill, piercing cry of unbearable anguish.

Her ears couldn't believe what they were hearing, and soon her eyes couldn't believe what they were seeing. Miss Meyers's desk began to vibrate—on its own! It rose a few inches off the floor and wobbled until pens, papers, and books spilled off of it. Seconds later the drawers on the teacher's file cabinet flew open on their own.

And through it all the moaning—that terrible, torturous shrieking—enveloped the entire room. Trying desperately to gather her wits, Brynn could feel the blood racing through her body. Struggling against paralyzing fear, Brynn finally forced out a scream of her own.

Just then Miss Meyers entered the room. "Brynn, what's the matter?"

Brynn rose from her seat and flew into her teacher's arms. Crying and trembling, Brynn cried, "Miss Meyers, that awful moaning sound returned. Your desk started shaking on its own. The file drawers opened by themselves and—"

"Brynn, stop, slow down, and catch your breath," Miss Meyers said calmly. "Everything is going to be all right." She held the frightened girl tightly. Whatever it was, the teacher knew, had scared the daylights out of Brynn.

When Brynn settled down, she noticed that the moaning had stopped. "You did hear it, didn't you?"

"I heard only you screaming," said Miss Meyers.

"Did you see the desk move?"

"No, Brynn. I see my things are on the floor, and the file cabinet is open. Do you know who did this?"

"No, Miss Meyers, I don't," said Brynn, still shaking. "I was sitting at my desk studying when that moaning—the same sound I heard last month—started up again. And then your desk moved by itself and so did the file cabinet." Brynn tugged on her teacher's arm. "I'm telling you the truth. Please believe me."

"Let's go down to the office and talk to Mr. Gordon."

"I don't want to talk to the principal," Brynn said, pulling away. "He'll think I did it, or else he'll think I'm crazy."

"No one will think you're crazy. It's obvious that something has scared you badly."

Later, gentle probing by Miss Meyers, Mr. Gordon, a school psychologist, and her mother convinced them that Brynn was not lying. She sincerely believed she was telling the truth. The psychologist concluded that Brynn suffered from a delusion caused by all the sudden changes in her life. As for any other explanation, the adults were at a loss.

"I'm not going back in that room," Brynn stated flatly. "It's haunted."

On the advice of the school psychologist, Mr. Gordon tried

to be understanding. "There's no reason to think it's haunted," countered the principal. "But, okay, Brynn, we'll move you into Mrs. Ford's class down the hall in Room 113."

"That's fine with me. I know you think I'm loony, but I never want to walk into Room 106 again."

"Let's just put this matter behind us, okay?"

But Brynn couldn't—not after what happened two weeks later.

Her class had just been let out for lunch. Students in the hallway were shuffling in and out of various rooms, clogging the hallway. Brynn had almost reached the cafeteria when she realized she had left her lunch bag back in her classroom. She worked her way through the crush of students and entered the now-empty room. She had taken only a few steps inside when she stood still.

Something doesn't feel right, she told herself. *What is it? I don't hear anything unusual. Hey, that's it! It's quiet—too quiet.* Her heart started to race from anxiety. *I don't hear anything at all!* No kids laughing, squealing, or chattering. No shoes clomping on the wood floor in the hallway. No traffic noise coming from outside the open window.

Suddenly, in the far corner of the room, a man—the most frightening person she had ever seen in her life—appeared out of nowhere. The man, in his twenties, stood about six feet (1.8 m) tall and had a muscular build. His wrinkled yellow shirt and jeans were caked with dried mud. Thick, matted brown hair that hadn't been washed for days nor cut in weeks was curled from sweat at the front and back of his head. The man's eyes—wild like a cornered animal—blazed with fury. His dirt-smeared, unshaven face was twisted into a hate that made Brynn's blood turn cold.

A thick rope was wrapped tightly around his neck. The rope ran down to his feet where it was tied around his weather-beaten boots. His wrists were bound with more rope in front of his waist. Slowly he raised his tied-up hands and, with his index fingers, pointed directly at the petrified girl.

"You, Missy Green, will pay for this," he hissed with a menacing sneer. "I will haunt you and your children, and your children's children, and their children. Beware—if they dare step foot over the ground of my last breath."

Reeling from absolute terror that left her light-headed, Brynn put her hands on the back of a desk to steady herself. Finally she sputtered, "But I'm not Missy Green."

"Mark my words, Missy, you and your descendants will pay for my death!"

Brynn recoiled in horror when flames burst forth in a deadly circle around the evil-eyed man. The fire licked at his boots before closing in on him. He emitted a low, steady moan that grew in pitch—the same vile groan that Brynn had heard twice before. It erupted into a horrifying screech as the blaze roared higher until it completely engulfed him. The dreadful wail soon was muffled by the crackling flames' dance of death.

The shell-shocked girl fled the room. From the hallway she waved her hands wildly and yelled, "Fire! Fire!"

As two teachers sprinted toward Brynn, she shouted, "In the corner of the room! A man is on fire!"

One of the teachers grabbed a fire extinguisher and dashed inside, but moments later returned, shaking his head and looking annoyed. "There is no fire," he announced. "And there is no man."

"There has to be," she argued. "I saw him. Flames were shooting up all around him."

The teacher led her inside and angrily demanded, "Do you see a fire anywhere? Do you see even a shred of evidence of a fire? Do you see anyone in here?"

Brynn backed away, totally bewildered. "I don't understand. I swear to you, I saw a man on fire."

By now more than a dozen students had rushed to the scene and crowded around the door, snickering at Brynn. "Man, she's lost it," said one student.

"She's gone off the deep end."

"Oh, is she in trouble now."

"Come with me, young lady," ordered the teacher, directing her through the crowd. "We're going to the principal's office."

Brynn was so upset by the incident that she refused to return to school. That was fine with Mr. Gordon, who, along with the school psychologist, was confident the girl suffered from a severe emotional problem.

Disturbed and worried, her mother took Brynn for therapy, where a psychiatrist all but convinced the girl that she had been seeing and hearing things that never existed. Deep inside herself, Brynn still believed that what she witnessed was real. *Why would I imagine such awful things? Why would I create this terrible scene in my mind? And who is Missy Green anyway?*

Everyone concerned, including Brynn, thought she would be better off in another school, so she transferred to Quincy Middle School. Fortunately Brynn never experienced another ghastly incident. No more eerie moans and groans, no more floating desk, no more evil-looking man in flames. By the end of the school year she seemed fine. But she always wondered what really happened.

Brynn never would have discovered the truth if she hadn't talked to Clover Willoughby, her great aunt, at a family reunion over the summer in Chicago. Clover, the sister of Brynn's maternal grandmother, was considered by most relatives to be slightly off center—a touch wacky. The 70-year-old believed in everything from ghosts to reincarnation to UFOs. She attended lectures and took adult education classes on the subjects. Her mind was as open as her mouth, which never stopped moving because she was constantly telling people about her latest interest. Most relatives listened politely before brushing her off.

At the reunion they paid her more attention than usual because she had helped prepare a detailed family tree on Brynn's mother's side. With mild interest Brynn examined the diagram of ancestors, spread out over 30 sheets of computer paper, taped to one of the walls of the hotel meeting room where the reunion was being held. Her eyes glanced over dozens of names of her ancestors, going back into the early 1800s, when . . .

"That's her!" Brynn shouted. "That's the one!" She blushed when she saw that everyone had stopped talking and was staring at her. "Um, sorry."

What was I going to say? she thought. *Gee, folks, I just came across the name of my great-great-great grandmother who happened to be mentioned by an evil-looking man who went up in flames in my classroom and who everyone thinks I invented. Give me a break. I've got to know more about her.*

She hustled over to Clover, pulled her aside, and begged, "Aunt Clover, tell me everything you know about Missy Green."

Thrilled that a member of the latest generation had taken such interest in the family tree, Clover offered Brynn a chair. Then she sat in one directly in front of the girl so their knees were practically touching.

"It's amazing that you should single out Missy Green," said Clover. "She's involved in an incredible story that goes way, way back to the mid-1800s. Your ancestors came from England and then headed west in a wagon train and stopped in, of all places, Spalding, Ohio, where they made their home for a while. They stayed in Spalding for about 20 years and then moved on to the Chicago area, where, for the most part, the family has grown and lived over the past 150 years. You and your mother are the first descendants to have returned to Spalding."

"What's so amazing about Missy Green?"

"Patience, my child, patience. I'm getting to that. Missy was one of four children born to Franklin and Dorothea Green. The Greens were fairly well off financially, and they built a big house on a hill overlooking the town square."

"That's where Bloom—the school I used to go to—is."

"Well, isn't that interesting? As I was saying, the Greens had some bucks and used to entertain a lot, throwing big parties with music and dancing and food. One night they were having a gala affair when a deputy came by and told the guests, 'Did you hear about the murder just across the river in West Virginia? A no-good thug robbed a bank and shot and killed a teller. The killer got away. Witnesses said he stole a horse, made it across the river, and might be somewhere in Spalding. Keep your eyes peeled.'

"And then someone said, 'Oh, my goodness. He might be in this very house. You never know.' The men at the party started joking and said that maybe one of the Green kids ought to search upstairs, just to make sure the killer wasn't hiding out. The children ranged in age from 6 to 12, and none of them were too keen on searching for a killer alone upstairs.

"Missy's daddy, Franklin Green, was a tough, fierce man who demanded that his kids fear nothing. So he said, 'The bravest child here will take a candle and go upstairs and look around.' Of course, he didn't really think a killer was in the house.

"He stared at Missy, who was only 10 years old. She had guts. Although she was scared, she didn't want to disappoint her father, so she stepped forward and said, 'I'll look for you, Papa.' Franklin beamed as he handed Missy a candle. Then he boasted, 'There never has been a Green yet who was a coward. Missy, go search the upstairs—and don't forget to check under the beds.'

"You can imagine how frightened a 10-year-old would be. She was shaking like a leaf, but she had spunk too. She went upstairs and peeked around the doors and then looked under the beds. Everything was fine until she stooped to check under her own bed. She lifted up the bedspread and held the candle low. And lo and behold, who do you suppose she was staring eyeball to eyeball with? None other than the killer himself!

"Well, she screamed so loud the house shook, and then she fainted. Her father and the others tore upstairs and wrestled with the killer. It turned out that he used to work for Franklin before he was fired for stealing. They tied him up from his neck to his feet and then tossed him into the basement. Meanwhile, they carried Missy downstairs and splashed water on her face until she regained consciousness.

"Wouldn't you know, Franklin Green demanded that they all go back to the party! And that's what they did, dancing up a storm. Supposedly, curiosity got the better of Missy, and she sneaked off and went into the basement to see the killer. He tried to sweet-talk her into believing that he wasn't the murderer and that he was only in the house to play a practical joke on her father.

"But she wasn't buying his story at all. She could tell by the evil in his eyes that he was bad news. She told him he was going to hang for his dastardly deed. As she was leaving, he put a curse on her: 'I will haunt you and your children, and your children's children, and their children.'"

Brynn gripped her chair because those familiar words triggered appalling memories of the evil man. She interrupted her aunt: "He then said, 'Beware if they dare step foot over the ground of my last breath.'"

"You've heard this story before?"

"No, Aunt Clover," replied Brynn, beginning to shake. "I'll explain everything later. So what happened next?"

"After he cursed Missy, she left and went back to the party. It was really going strong when the ceiling caught on fire! The whole second floor had become engulfed in flames. Apparently, when Missy found the killer upstairs and screamed, she dropped her lit candle, and it rolled on the floor under the drapes. In all the confusion that followed, no one noticed. After they all had gone downstairs, the candle flame ignited the drapes, which smoldered for a while before the fire spread. With all the partying going on downstairs, no one knew the fire was raging upstairs until it was too late.

"Everybody fled the house, and they forgot all about the killer, who was tied up in the basement—that is, until they heard him moaning and groaning. He was screaming in agony, but there was nothing anyone could do. They weren't about to risk their lives to save him—especially a killer who was going to be hanged anyway. His screams finally stopped when the house collapsed in a fiery heap. They later found his body in the ashes. Nobody shed a tear for the killer, that's for sure.

"Because the Greens were wealthy, they rebuilt the house—only instead of using wood they put up a fine brick mansion. And here's the spooky part. Every night at the same time the killer died in the basement, Missy Green could hear him moaning and groaning. No one else heard him. Only Missy Green. They thought she was going crazy. Well, eventually, the Greens moved to Chicago, and no one ever heard those moans and groans again."

"I wouldn't be so sure about that, Aunt Clover," said Brynn, her voice cracking.

Seeing a swirl of emotions in Brynn's eyes, her aunt asked, "Honey, what's bothering you?"

Brynn then told Clover her terrible ordeals at Bloom Middle School—the strange moaning, the moving furniture, and the man in flames. "Why would I be the only one to see and hear him? Why would he call me Missy Green? Why did it happen? Or *did* it even happen?"

Clover folded her arms and bit on her lower lip while she slipped into deep thought. Then she announced, "It definitely happened, Brynn. It all makes sense. His curse was on Missy Green's descendants—and you're one of them. Remember the other part of the curse: 'Beware if they dare step foot over the ground of my last breath.'

"Missy was haunted by the killer because she lived in the rebuilt house over the spot where he died. Soon the Greens moved out of Spalding. From then on, for over a century, neither Missy nor any of her descendants ever lived in

Spalding, so they weren't haunted. But then you and your mom moved there."

Brynn bent over and squeezed her aunt's knee because she finally understood. "The haunting started up again at my school—because it was built where Missy's house used to be! And I am Missy's descendant!"

"Exactly, my child."

Brynn broke down in sobs. Out of relief—and out of fear. She felt relieved because she hadn't been crazy after all. What she heard and saw in school was the killer's ghost and the result of his vicious curse. But then Brynn felt fearful for the very same reasons. It was all so shockingly true.

From that day on, Brynn Slater never came within a block of Bloom Middle School. No one in the family could blame her. And she was never haunted again.

THE SCENE-STEALER

The lanky boy in the wide-brimmed hat, western shirt, blue jeans, and cowboy boots sauntered out into the middle of the stage, lit only by a lone spotlight. He began to prance in slow motion as if he were learning the steps to a dance number. He looked out of place, because the set on the stage was that of a mansion in England for the musical *My Fair Lady*.

In the back of the otherwise darkened and empty theater at Taft High School, drama teacher Michael Drabek told janitor Charley Clayton, "I thought everyone was gone."

"They were," Charley replied. "I checked before turning off all the lights, including the ones onstage." The janitor then called out to the boy, "Excuse me, young man! It's time to leave!"

The teen didn't miss a beat. He continued with his quiet dance routine, ignoring the janitor. Charley began to walk toward the stage when Mr. Drabek gently held him by the arm and whispered, "Let's watch him for a moment."

Onstage the boy broke out into song: "Oh, what a

beautiful morning. Oh, what a beautiful day. I've got a beautiful feeling, everything's going my way . . . ."

"He's doing a song and dance number from the musical *Oklahoma*," Mr. Drabek noted.

"You're right," said the janitor, who had seen every production that the Taft High drama students had put on since he began working at the school in 1986. "He's playing Curly, the lead role. The drama department did *Oklahoma* my first year on the job—long before you took over as drama instructor."

"He's not bad," said Mr. Drabek. "I can't tell who he is, though. Not enough light."

"Hey, kid!" the janitor yelled again. "No one is supposed to be in here now. We're locking up the theater."

The cowboy finished his song with a flourish and then jumped off the stage onto the center aisle. The moment his feet touched the floor, the lone spotlight that had been shining on the stage went out. Charley immediately flipped on the houselights, but the boy was gone. The teacher and janitor looked for him down each row without any luck.

"That's odd," said Mr. Drabek. "We saw him jump off the stage. He had to go past us to get out of the theater."

"He simply disappeared," said Charley. "If I didn't know better, I'd say we're the first people to witness a performance by the Taft High Theater's resident ghost."

Mr. Drabek, who was in his first year at Taft, had heard about the ghost but didn't really believe in it. He chalked it up to a legend kept alive by students and staff who enjoyed spreading the story of a friendly spirit roaming the school's theater.

Although no one claimed to have seen the ghost, several students reported feeling his presence. In 1988 one actress who was struggling through rehearsals revealed that she felt a ghost gently push her into a different position and guide her around the stage. Her performances improved so much that the spirit patted her on the back.

During auditions a year later a nervous student felt unseen hands help him around the stage. He landed the part, but the hands still steered him through rehearsals.

Then there was the time a few years back when one of the actresses accidentally knocked over a vase of fresh "good luck" flowers in the dressing room. Water and flowers had spilled onto the floor, but before she could clean it up she was ordered out onto the stage. As she headed out the door she turned around and, to her amazement, saw the flowers back in the vase.

Over the years stagehands reported hearing someone walking on the catwalk above the stage during rehearsals. At other times spotlights inexplicably would turn on and off by themselves—but only when rehearsals weren't going well.

That night in 1991 when Mr. Drabek and Charley watched a mysterious cowboy perform was the first time the theater ghost was actually seen.

The following year the spirit made an even more impressive showing. He appeared after students had finished rehearsing for *Grease,* a musical about high school life in the 1950s. Only a few kids were hanging around the stage with Mr. Drabek when, from the back of the theater, they heard a voice launch into song.

"I'm a Yankee doodle dandy, a Yankee doodle do or die.

A real life nephew of my Uncle Sam, born on the Fourth of July . . ."

The people onstage covered their eyes to block the glare from the stage lights and peered out into the empty audience. They spotted a lanky boy in a floppy blue cap pulled down low over his face. He had on a red, white, and blue striped shirt, red suspenders, and blue pants with white stars going up the legs. He tap-danced down the center aisle toward the stage, twirled, and worked his way back. All the while he sang with gusto in a voice that echoed off the walls of the theater.

The students and Mr. Drabek watched as the young man sang and danced with remarkable ease and skill. When they lost him in the shadows near the back of the theater, the students and teacher broke out in applause.

"Very good, whoever you are!" shouted Mr. Drabek. "Come on down for an encore."

The teacher and the rest of the students waited for the boy to reveal himself. But after a minute of silence and no movement coming from the dimly lit theater, Mr. Drabek asked Charley to turn up the houselights. When they became brighter, the drama teacher scanned the rows of empty chairs. "Hey, where did you go?" Turning to those onstage, he asked, "Did you see where he went?" They all shook their heads.

"The doors in the back didn't open, so he has to be around here somewhere," said Charley. "He was doing a number from the musical *George M*, about the life of songwriter George M. Cohan. I remember the play was done here a few years ago."

After a futile search Mr. Drabek asked the students, "Does anybody know who he is?"

He received nothing but blank stares until Keesha Lane, one of his students, spoke up. "You may think I'm nuts, but I believe it was the theater ghost."

"You're probably right," said the teacher.

"So you think this place is haunted?"

"No, I think you're nuts," the teacher joked.

SLAM . . . SLAM . . . SLAM . . . SLAM . . . SLAM.

Startled, everyone stared out into the audience. Normally, the cushioned seats of the theater chairs were automatically folded up when they were unoccupied. But scattered throughout the rows, a dozen seats were in the down position.

"The seats moved by themselves!" claimed one of the stunned students.

"See, Mr. Drabek, I bet the theater ghost did it," said Keesha.

"I'm not convinced," insisted the teacher. "But I admit I can't come up with a better explanation at the moment."

"It's interesting," said Charley, "that his size and voice are pretty much those of the cowboy we saw last year, Mr. Drabek."

"You know, you're right. He's a good dancer. And his voice, why, it's one of the best I've heard from a high school student."

"If indeed he is a student," Charley noted.

The following year, during rehearsals for a production of *South Pacific*, a musical set on the island of Bali, Mr. Drabek and student Jasmine Peters were cuing up tape recordings of various sound effects from a control room off the stage. When the rehearsal was over, they closed and locked the control room. As they walked out they heard a young man's powerful voice singing, "Luck, be a lady tonight. Luck, be a lady tonight. Luck, if you've ever been a lady to begin with, Luck, be a lady tonight."

"That's from the musical *Guys and Dolls*," said Mr. Drabek. "One of the lead characters, a gambler named Sky Masterson, is singing to a pair of dice."

"Whoever is singing," said Jasmine, "he's terrific."

"That voice sounds familiar." A chill crept up the teacher's spine. It sounded exactly like the mystery performer's voice! "The singing is coming over the sound system."

They opened the door to the control room and found the reel-to-reel tape recorder was playing. "I thought you turned off the tape machine," said Mr. Drabek.

"I did. You saw me do it."

The teacher shut it off. "Why would that voice be on this sound-effects tape?"

"It shouldn't be," Jasmine replied. "We both listened to the entire tape and picked out the special effects we wanted. We didn't hear anyone singing on it before."

Mr. Drabek rewound the tape and played it again. This time they heard the sound effects only, no singing. So he turned off the tape machine and locked the door to the control room. No sooner had they stepped away when the voice came through the sound system again, singing, "Luck, be a lady tonight . . ."

The teacher dashed back into the control room and pointed to the tape player. It was on again—and playing the song that didn't exist on the tape!

"I'm about ready to admit that the theater ghost exists after all," Mr. Drabek said with a sigh.

❋   ❋   ❋

Of the two major student productions a year that Mr. Drabek directed, one was always a musical. One day, a year after his previous encounter with the ghost, the teacher was unlocking his office door and wondering what new musical to select. Inside he discovered that a shelf that held stacks of scripts had collapsed during the night, spilling them all over the floor.

As he picked them up, his eye caught the title of one of the scripts, *Bye-Bye, Birdie. Hmm,* he thought. *It has lots of fun songs, it's about an Elvis Presley-type star headed for the army, and it involves high school fans. That's perfect. We'll do it. I'll call for open auditions next month.*

At the auditions he picked several students for key parts, but was unsure about who to cast for the title role. With the stage nearly bare and most everyone heading home, the teacher was about to call an end to the auditions.

From the left side of the stage a lanky boy of 17 appeared. Mr. Drabek thought he looked familiar but couldn't quite place him. With his head down the teen shuffled forward and mumbled, "I'd like to, uh, audition, sir, if you don't mind, that is."

Oh, brother, thought Mr. Drabek. *He lacks confidence and stage presence. But I'd better give him a chance anyway. It looks like it was a big effort for him to find the courage to step forward. I'd hate to wreck his confidence.* Not expecting much from the somewhat timid young man, the teacher said, "Okay, let's hear what you've got."

Speaking in a halting, barely audible voice, the boy said, "This is, uh, the song where Conrad Birdie kisses the, um, girl who was selected to represent all fans. She, uh, gives him a good-bye kiss before, um, he heads off into the army."

Mrs. Roberts, the pianist, began to play, and suddenly the bashful boy transformed right before everyone's eyes into a dynamic rock star. Crouching down low, he flashed a racy sneer and a leering gaze meant to be funny. Then he leaped up and belted out a tune that left everyone in openmouthed amazement. "One last kiss, oh, give me one last kiss. It never felt like this. No, never felt like this . . ."

He gyrated across the stage, jumping and twirling, and topped off his comic performance by mugging in the exaggerated style of a rock star. Most impressive of all, his voice filled the theater with its clarity, power, and passion.

That voice sounds so alive, so vibrant . . . so familiar, thought Mr. Drabek.

Students who had been walking out of the theater turned around and crowded the front of the stage, watching with envy as the teen delivered a dynamic performance. When he finished everyone broke out in applause.

"That was fantastic!" declared Mr. Drabek. "Now *that's* entertainment!"

The boy bowed, flashed a wide grin, and said politely, "Thank you, sir, thank you very much. I appreciate your kind words." He bowed again as he walked backward toward the left side of the stage.

"You captured the role perfectly. You *were* Conrad Birdie!" Mr. Drabek continued to heap praise until he realized that the young man had backed away to the edge of the curtain.

"Wait, where are you going?" asked Mr. Drabek. "Come over here. What's your name?"

The boy slipped out of sight behind the curtain. Mr. Drabek leaped off his seat in the front row, hopped onto the stage, and ran after him. The teacher brushed back the curtain and bumped into a student. "Where is the boy who just auditioned?"

"I don't know," came the reply. "I was walking onto the stage and didn't see anyone go past me."

"That's impossible," said Mr. Drabek. "I saw him leave this way—" Suddenly the teacher's eyes caught sight of a plaque beyond the student's shoulder. "This can't be."

Mr. Drabek walked up to the plaque and studied it carefully. It was bronze and bolted into the wall next to the control room. It read, "In Memory of Our Beloved Son, Christopher Fairly, 1967–1984." Above the words was an etching of Chris's face—looking exactly like the young man who had performed so brilliantly in the audition. *Now I know where I've seen that face before,* thought Mr. Drabek. *I walk past this plaque almost every day.*

With trembling hands Mr. Drabek let his fingers glide over the plaque. Goose bumps appeared on his arms. *Could Chris Fairly be the ghost of the Taft High Theater? And if so, why did he make himself so visible today?*

The next day the teacher went to the media center and looked up the 1984-85 Taft High School yearbook. Near the front was a page dedicated to Chris Fairly. A small article read: "The school was saddened by the tragic death of junior Christopher Fairly. Chris, a member of the drama club, was practicing for an upcoming audition for the role of Conrad Birdie in the musical *Bye-Bye, Birdie* when a curtain rope holding a 50-pound weight snapped. The weight fell down and struck Chris on the head. He died two days later in the hospital from severe head injuries. His fellow students will miss him very much."

Accompanying the passage was a black-and-white photo

of a smiling teen. There was now no longer any doubt in Mr. Drabek's mind. The boy who auditioned the day before—who over the previous years had performed with such vigor—was none other than the ghost of Christopher Fairly!

Later that day the teacher shared his astounding conclusion with Charley the janitor. "Charley," the teacher said excitedly. "I think I have it figured out. I went through the yearbooks over the last ten years. There was a period from the fall of 1986 until I took over as the drama instructor 1991 when there were no musicals performed at the Taft High Theater.

"Chris's ghost made his presence known during rehearsals of dramas and comedies, but no one ever saw him until you and I did in 1991. He performed only during rehearsals of musicals from then on. I wondered why he didn't sing a song from any of the musicals we were producing. Instead he did songs from *Oklahoma, George M, Guys and Dolls,* and *Bye-Bye, Birdie.* It just so happens that these four musicals were put on at the Taft High Theater during what would have been his junior and senior years had he not been killed. Charley, Chris's ghost was singing songs for the roles that he had hoped to play had he lived!"

"He did a wonderful job, Mr. Drabek, but he always kept his face hidden from everyone. So why did he show his face at this latest audition?"

"Because for the first time since his death the school was doing the very same musical that he had planned to perform in. On the day he died he was preparing to audition for the part of Conrad Birdie. He finally got the chance to try out for the title role."

"Do you think we'll see his ghost again?"

"I doubt it, Charley. I believe his spirit stuck around until he found the proof that he was looking for."

"What proof was that?"

"That he was good enough to be the star of the show. And you know what, Charley? He was more than good enough. He was great!"

THE RED-ROCK SPIRITS

The five barefoot children—three boys and two girls of grade-school age—squealed with laughter as they chased each other around a huge jagged red boulder in an otherwise barren sandlot. But then the wind kicked up, forcing the kids to dodge swirling "dust devils" and bounding balls of tumbleweed. Nevertheless the game of tag continued . . . until a little girl screamed in terror. The other kids stopped playing, and horror quickly spread across their faces. And then came total darkness.

For three nights in a row the same dreadful dream haunted 15-year-old Jose Dilone. Each time he woke up in a cold sweat and asked himself, *Why am I having this awful nightmare? Who are these kids? What's scaring them? What does this dream mean?*

Within a week Jose would discover the shocking truth.

Jose first had the nightmare right after he started a summer job as a laborer for his uncle, Maximillian "Maxi" Cortez. Maxi owned a demolition company that had the task of tearing down the old Red Rock Elementary School, which had outlived its usefulness. After nearly 80 years the school had shown its age—a roof of crumbling orange barrel tiles and walls of cracked, weather-stained white stucco. The two-story building would soon be replaced by a new sprawling elementary school for the growing town of Hildago, California.

Jose never attended Red Rock, but it soon would make a lasting impact on his life. The teen had hung around with the wrong crowd in his sophomore year in high school and tended to be a bit lazy. He wasn't too thrilled when his parents ordered him to spend the summer with his strict, no-nonsense uncle. They thought physical labor would trigger an attitude adjustment in their son and keep him out of trouble.

But during the first days on the job, Jose tried to slack off whenever he could, by catching a few winks in an empty classroom or behind a bulldozer. After ignoring several warnings from the foreman, Jose was called into the trailer that was used as the company office for the project.

"Listen to me, young man," Uncle Maxi said, his eyes glaring. "I am paying you a decent wage, and I expect decent work from you in return. Just because you're my nephew doesn't give you the right to goof off. I'm not here to be your baby-sitter."

"But it's hard, boring work."

"That's too bad. I expect nothing less from you than I expect from my own men. They work very, very hard. We've all got a job to do. Now do yours. Do you understand?"

Jose stared at the floor and shrugged.

"Look at me when I'm talking to you!" Uncle Maxi barked. "And answer me clearly."

Startled, Jose raised his head and mumbled, "Yes, sir."

"I didn't hear you."

"Yes, sir!" Jose shouted.

"Good, now get to work."

Jose and his cousin Nando Cortez—Maxi's son—went inside the school gymnasium to salvage the hardwood floors by prying up strips of oak. Minutes after they started, the boys heard the faint sound of children chanting, "The day is done, ain't no foolin'. . . . No more books, no more schoolin'."

"Did you hear that?" asked Nando.

"Sounds like some kids sneaked in here," Jose said.

"They shouldn't be in the school. Let's go find them before they get hurt." Nando and Jose searched each of the ten rooms on the first floor but found no evidence of the kids. The two workers returned to the gym. Soon they heard the childish chants again.

"They're upstairs," said Jose. As the teens bounded up the stairs they could hear the chants more clearly. "They must be in this room," Jose said, approaching Room 201. But when he walked in, the room was empty.

"Where are they?" asked Nando.

"I don't get it. The singing definitely came from this room."

Jose glanced at the blackboard where a drawing of a stick figure was hanging from a gallows with several blanks and letters underneath that read: _ E _ _ O C _ .

"Hey, look at this," said Jose. "It's the game hangman." He picked up a piece of chalk and filled in the blanks so the letters spelled RED ROCK. "Yep, Red Rock is about to face its doom."

"Those kids will face some trouble if we ever find them," said Nando. "They probably did this. They're turning this into a game of 'catch us if you can.'"

"We'll catch them," Jose pledged. "They're not going to make fools out of us."

The boys left the room and checked the other classrooms on the second floor without finding any signs of the elusive children. As the teens headed for the stairway, they heard a squeaky, scratching noise. "Sounds like chalk on a blackboard," Nando whispered, signaling Jose to keep quiet. He pointed to Room 201, where they suspected the kids were writing on the blackboard.

The boys tiptoed to the entrance of the classroom. Nando nodded, and the two leaped into the room, expecting to catch the kids. But to the teens' surprise the room was still empty.

"I don't get it," said Nando. "I was positive the kids were here."

Jose shook his head in bewilderment. Then his eyes focused on the blackboard and the letters beneath the hanging stick figure. "Very funny, Nando."

"What?"

"Look at the letters."

"Wow! They spell DILONE—your name."

"So who did it?" Jose muttered. "One of the other workers? That's it, isn't it? You and the others are pulling my leg, right?"

"I had nothing to do with this, Jose. Maybe it was one of those kids."

"How would they know my name? And where are they?" His hand swept across the empty room. "There's no place to hide in here."

117

Nando shrugged. He had no answer.

As they headed downstairs, the boys could hear the kids giggling. Jose started to fume. "They're having fun at our expense," he griped. "Wait until I get my hands on those little punks. Let's split up. We'll have a better chance of catching them."

Jose stomped into the boys' bathroom and searched the stalls. As he started to leave he looked at the cracked mirror. In the reflection he noticed a small boy about ten years old in bare feet, no shirt, and dirty gray pants that looked too big for his size. The only thing keeping the baggy pants on his thin body was a leather belt with a huge silver buckle in the shape of a bull. Jose glanced up from the unusual silver buckle and into the boy's eyes, which twinkled under a thatch of thick black hair. A wide grin revealed a missing front tooth.

"Aha!" Jose shouted triumphantly, turning around. "You're not getting away . . . hey, where did you go?"

The boy was not there.

Jose checked the stalls again and then scurried out of the bathroom and bumped into Nando. "Did you see a boy run out of here?"

"No," Nando replied.

"I saw a barefoot kid in the bathroom, and then he disappeared."

"Jose, there's no way anyone could have come out of the bathroom without me seeing him."

"Jose! Nando! Where are you?"

"Oh-oh," said Jose. "It's Uncle Maxi."

The boys rushed back into the gym, where Maxi gave them a tongue-lashing. "Why is it that every time I come in here, you two are gone?"

"But, Uncle Maxi, we heard kids in the building."

"*Kids?* There are no children in here. The area is completely fenced off. No one can sneak in here without someone spotting them first. The only children in here are you two. Now get back to work! *Pronto!*"

That night Jose had the nightmare again. He woke up from the dream right when the kids began screaming. Only this time he was thunderstruck by a stunning discovery. "Oh, my gosh," he shouted out loud from his bed. "The boy I saw in the bathroom mirror was one of the kids in my dream!"

The next day he and Nando had finished tearing up the gym flooring and stacking the wood outside when they heard the faint sounds of children in a classroom. The kids were reciting, "Two times two is four. Two times three is six. Two times four is eight."

"It's those kids again," said Jose. "Let's see if we can sneak up on them."

He and Nando crept slowly down the hall as the children's voices grew louder. "Two times five is ten. Two times six is twelve."

"We've got them now," whispered Jose. To Nando he silently mouthed, "One, two, three." The two sprang into the classroom. "Aha!" he yelled. "We got you!" But the only ones in the room were Nando and Jose.

"This is crazy," muttered Jose. "The kids definitely were in this room. We heard them."

"Jose, look at the blackboard." Scrawled in big letters were the chalked words "DON'T DO IT!!!"

"That wasn't there yesterday," said Jose.

Nando pounded the wall in frustration and raged, "Those

kids are still playing games with us!"

Perplexed by the strange events of the last two days, the boys hurried to the trailer office and told Uncle Maxi about the weird things going on inside the school. After hearing the boys' story, Maxi snapped, "I think you're both crazy. After the lunch break I want you to get busy and help Sanchez take the copper flashing off the roof."

More tired than hungry, Jose climbed into the seat of a bulldozer parked under a shade tree, leaned back, and caught a catnap. No sooner had he fallen asleep than he experienced the nightmare again. At the point where the kids in the dream always shrieked in terror, Jose woke up by tumbling out of the seat. As he picked himself up he noticed the other workers were laughing at him.

"Okay, everyone, let's get back to work," growled Uncle Maxi. "Fun's over." He motioned for Jose to come over and then he whispered angrily to the teen, "Quit embarrassing me. Now get up on the roof with Sanchez and Nando."

"Uncle Maxi, I had a bad dream and—"

"Then quit sleeping on the job! Now get on that roof. *Pronto!*"

After Nando and Sanchez had climbed up, Jose was scaling the ladder when it began vibrating. "Nando," Jose said, "quit playing with the ladder."

"I'm not. I thought you were."

"Oh, no!" Jose cried out. "Look! The ladder is hopping up and down—on its own!" Jose clutched onto the sides, wondering whether to jump down 12 feet (3.6 m) to the concrete sidewalk below. But the ladder was shaking so violently that he was afraid he would get hurt if he tried to jump.

"Hang on, Jose!" shouted Nando. Cupping his hands, Nando yelled from atop the roof, "Help! Help!"

The other workers rushed over and then froze in astonishment. The angled ladder was literally hopping on its own and bouncing off the edge of the roof while Jose held on for dear life. Finally two workers grabbed the ladder. The bizarre dancing ladder slowed to a stop, allowing Jose to scramble down safely.

"What happened?" demanded Uncle Maxi.

"The ladder had a mind of its own," blurted his shaken nephew. "Uncle Maxi, I'm getting spooked—"

He was interrupted by children's laughter coming from a second-floor window. Through the filthy, cracked windows, five young kids—three boys and two girls—pointed at the workers below and giggled.

"There they are!" shouted Jose. "Those are the kids I've been talking about!" And then it dawned on him. *I've seen them before! They're the very kids in my nightmares!* He didn't have time to think further. Acting on his uncle's orders, Jose and the other workers charged up the stairs hoping to catch the trespassing children. The workers then fanned out and combed every square inch of the school, but just as Jose had expected—and feared—the search proved futile.

"There's no sign of them anywhere," the befuddled foreman told Maxi. "I don't know how they could have slipped past us, but they did."

Jose was the last one out of the building. When he joined the others, he looked pale and shaky. He held up a piece of wood in his trembling left hand and said, "This fell from the ceiling and hit me on the head." The words "GO AWAY!!!" were scrawled in red chalk.

"Uncle Maxi, I think this place is haunted," Jose declared. "Those kids must be ghosts."

"Ghost kids? Now I've heard everything!"

"Maxi," piped in Sanchez, "we all heard kids singing and laughing, and then they disappeared."

"And we saw what happened to Jose on the ladder," added the foreman.

"And there's this," remarked Nando, pointing to an exterior gym wall where another "GO AWAY!!!" message was painted on the side. "That wasn't there a minute ago."

"Well, it won't be there for long!" declared Maxi. The fuming boss hopped into the seat of the bulldozer and started up the engine. "Get out of my way, men!" He thrust the machine in gear, and the bulldozer lurched toward the gym wall that Maxi was determined to knock down. But then, only a few feet from the school, the bulldozer's engine sputtered and died. Maxi tried to start it up again, but the engine refused to turn over.

Maxi leaped down, whipped off his cap, and threw it to the ground in disgust. He stared at his men and then bellowed, "Well, don't just stand there! Get going! We've got a school to tear down!"

Reluctantly the men climbed onto the other two bulldozers, three endloaders, and two trucks. But, incredibly, when they tried to start them, none of the machinery would run.

"Uncle Maxi," said Jose, "I'm telling you this school is haunted!"

Some of the other men began mumbling in agreement. "Maxi," said one of them, "I don't like the feel of this place. I'm leaving."

"Me too," said a worker. A few more men nodded in agreement and walked off the job.

"Anyone who takes one more step is fired!" Maxi thundered.

"Go ahead," said another employee. "Fire me if you have to, but I'm not working with ghosts in the school."

Minutes later his crew was cut in half, down to eight men. Maxi glared at Jose and then stormed off into the trailer. He phoned a mechanic, who came out and checked the machinery. In every case, wires had mysteriously been pulled out or switched, which caused the engines to fail.

Meanwhile Jose felt a need to walk through the school again. Filled with a mixture of fear and curiosity, he went into the room where he first had heard the kids. He didn't know why, but he placed his hands firmly on a wall as if the school building were alive, and he was trying to feel its pulse.

Jose began to hear the kids' voices. But they weren't coming from inside the school. They were coming from inside his *head*! Frightened by this latest twist, Jose wanted to flee, but a stronger force kept him rooted in the room. Looking like a burglar who had been caught by a cop, Jose faced the wall with his sweat-soaked forehead and quivering hands pressed against the wall.

He then experienced the most eerie yet realistic daydream of his life. He could see the faces of the five children—the same ones in his nightmare, the same ones in the upstairs window minutes earlier. Each one talked to him: "We like it here. This is our home." . . . "We want you to leave." . . . "Don't tear the school down." . . . "Go away." . . . "Leave us alone, or you'll be sorry."

Jose shoved himself away from the wall and cradled his

head. "What's the matter with me?" he cried. "Uncle Maxi is right. I must be crazy!"

He bolted out of the school and nearly bowled Maxi over. "Uncle Maxi," he said breathlessly. "The ghosts—"

"Stop with that nonsense!" Maxi ordered.

"But I've seen them. I've heard them. They gave me messages."

Although Maxi was annoyed, he decided to play along with his upset nephew. "What do they want?"

"They want us to leave," replied Jose. "This is their home. They don't want us to tear the school down. How would you like it if someone came and tried to wreck your home?"

"You're talking like a nut. Listen to me, Jose. We have a job to do, ghosts or no ghosts. Our machines are up and running, and it's time to bring this school down. Now grab a sledgehammer and knock down any parts of the wall that the big machines don't get."

Jose shook his head. "I can't go near the school anymore. I've got a sickening feeling that something terrible is going to happen."

"Well, guess what," Maxi hissed. "Something terrible is going to happen to you if you don't get back to work. We're behind schedule. And now that half the workers left because of all your talk about ghosts, I need you. Now move!"

With a feeling of impending doom, Jose picked up a sledgehammer and walked alongside the bulldozers as they rumbled toward the gymnasium wall. The machines plowed into the first wall, and it collapsed into a dusty heap of stucco and cement block.

Jose stepped up and halfheartedly raised his sledge-hammer to knock over a three-foot chunk of wall that remained standing. But just as he was ready to smash into the stucco, he felt an invisible force yank on the sledgehammer from behind.

While trying to understand who or what had stopped his swing, Jose heard his uncle shout with alarm, "Jose! Behind you! Get out of the way! Run, run!"

Jose wheeled around and saw that a large section of an adjoining wall was toppling toward him. He dropped his sledgehammer and tried to dart out of the way. But he tripped over the debris and his hard hat went flying as the wall collapsed on top of him. Then everything went black.

The five barefoot children squeal with laughter and chase each other around a huge, jagged red rock. The wind kicks up dust and blows the tumbleweed. Then a little girl screams in terror. The kids stop playing, and their giggles turn into shrieks of horror. The ground rumbles and rolls before heaving violently. The children scurry every which way in panic. They don't know what to do or where to go. The earth cracks open, and the ground directly under their feet tilts so steeply that the fear-stricken children slide toward a gaping hole. Clawing desperately at the dirt, they tumble into the darkness. The little gap-toothed boy with the silver bull-shaped belt buckle is the last to slip away. With cruel swiftness the ground closes up. All that marks the spot where the kids are swallowed up is the top third of the red rock.

A long time passes before construction begins on a building. The workers decide not to remove the jagged boulder, so they build the foundation around it. The building is two stories tall, with white stucco walls and red barrel tile. It is called Red Rock Elementary.

Over the years the spirits of the five children find joy and comfort inside the walls of the school. They thrive from the creative energy of its students and teachers. But then the peace becomes shattered by the roar of bulldozers and the crashing of walls.

"Jose, can you hear me? Can you open your eyes?"

Jose blinked several times and tried to focus on the fuzzy face of a stranger dressed in pale blue.

"Huh?" he said groggily. "Where am I? Who are you?"

"I'm Dr. Williams," said the physician. "You're in Hildago Hospital. You got conked on the head pretty good."

"Doctor," said Jose, "I know what happened."

"Yes, you suffered a bad concussion when the wall toppled over on you."

"No, that's not what I mean. I know what happened to the children, and why their ghosts have stayed at the school."

"Ghosts, huh? Why don't you get more rest."

Two days later, after Jose was released from the hospital, he visited the school. When he arrived he saw only rubble. The building had been leveled. With a heavy heart he solemnly walked around the chunks of crushed and broken stucco, assuming he would never see or hear the ghosts of the five children again. He then began picking through the debris, hoping to find the big jagged boulder to further convince him that his dreams were real.

"It's good to see you on your feet, Jose," said Maxi as he hugged his nephew. "You really gave us a scare."

"Uncle Maxi, did this area ever get hit by a bad earthquake?"

"That's a strange question to ask me after just getting out of the hospital. But, yes, I heard that about 80 years ago there was a terrible quake. It killed hundreds of people. Why do you ask?"

"Nothing, just wondered. I'll be back at work tomorrow."

"Really? That's great. Looks like that bop on the head may have knocked some sense into you!"

The next day, as the rubble was piled into dump trucks, an end loader was scooping up the debris when the shovel struck a boulder protruding from the ground inside the foundation walls.

That could be the red rock I saw in my dreams, thought Jose. He began tirelessly shoving chunks of stucco out of the way to get a better look. As he stepped back he could clearly see its red color and jagged shape. *That's the rock! The kids must be buried right next to it.*

After work, when everyone went home, Jose remained at the site. He grabbed a shovel and carefully dug around the boulder, not sure what he might find, but hoping it would prove the truth of his nightmares. After two hours of scooping, Jose unearthed something hard and gray. He reached deep into the dirt and pulled out the object—a tarnished silver belt buckle shaped like a bull.

As he held it in his trembling hands he dropped to his knees. *It's true!* he told himself. *It's all true! The kids I saw in the school were the ghosts of those who died in an earthquake on this very spot! They talked to me! Those poor kids. What a terrible way to die. And then to have their spirits upset by tearing down their school. What should I do now?*

Jose sat on the red rock for an hour and pondered his next course of action. Finally he placed the silver belt buckle back into the deep hole he had just dug and covered it with dirt.

"I'm sorry we tore down the school," Jose said, staring down at the freshly covered hole. "But I think you'll be happy once the new school is built. You'll be with students and teachers again."

Today, Red Rock Elementary features airy and bright classrooms, an impressive media center, and a neat cafeteria. Students and teachers love the school. But there is something eerie about it. Every once in a while—usually on a weekend or a holiday—a member of the faculty or office staff hears unseen children chanting, "The day is done, ain't no foolin'. . . . No more books, no more schoolin'."